HIT THE ROAD

Also by Caroline B. Cooney

The Janie books
The Face on the Milk Carton
Whatever Happened to Janie?
The Voice on the Radio
What Janie Found

The Time Travel Quartet
Both Sides of Time
Out of Time
Prisoner of Time
For All Time

Other books
Diamonds in the Shadow
A Friend at Midnight
Code Orange
The Girl Who Invented Romance
Family Reunion
Goddess of Yesterday
The Ransom of Mercy Carter
Tune In Anytime
Burning Up
What Child Is This?
Driver's Ed
Twenty Pageants Later
Among Friends

HIT
THE
ROAD

CAROLINE B. COONEY

LAUREL-LEAF BOOKS

Published by Laurel-Leaf
an imprint of Random House Children's Books
a division of Random House, Inc.
New York

Originally published in hardcover in the United States by
Delacorte Press, New York, in 2006. This edition published by
arrangement with Delacorte Press.

Laurel-Leaf and colophon are registered trademarks of
Random House, Inc.

www.randomhouse.com/teens

Educators and librarians, for a variety of teaching tools,
visit us at www.randomhouse.com/teachers

RL: 5.4
ISBN: 978-0-440-22929-2
January 2008
Printed in the United States of America
10 9 8 7 6 5 4 3
First Laurel-Leaf Edition

For my sister-in-law, Abigail Jane Bruce,
friend and driver

CHAPTER 1

Brit's family was the only one-car family in Connecticut. Brit had had her driver's license eleven days, and since there were now three drivers at her house, simple math meant three cars, or at least two. But instead of leaving their perfectly good car at home for Brit to drive around and enjoy, Mom and Dad were wasting it on an airport parking lot. Brit would be staying with Nannie while her parents were gone, but she couldn't even drive her grandmother's old Cadillac, because Mom had decided that Nannie was too old to drive and sold the Caddy to make absolutely sure Nannie couldn't go anywhere. Brittany Anne Bowman was going to be carless (very close to lifeless) for two weeks. She had texted every single friend she'd ever had—and plenty of people who weren't exactly friends but had been in class with her forever—that if they were going anywhere at all, they had to take her, because she would be desperate.

When Brit and her parents got to Nannie's house that morning, Nannie was standing outside in the rain, holding her handbag and looking around the front yard as if she were shopping at the mall. "Didn't I tell you?" Mom said. "She's losing her marbles."

"She is not losing her marbles!" said Brit, who adored her grandmother and hated when Mom said Nannie was failing. Nannie was wearing a mauve silk suit and looked rather like a tulip. To protect her stiffly curled white hair, she was holding a tan umbrella with PBS logos.

Brit's mother shouted to penetrate Nannie's deafness. "We're early, Mother! I'm worried about traffic. Here's Brit."

"I told you I cannot keep Brit this week," said her grandmother.

"Nannie!" said Brit, hurt.

"I reminded you twice," yelled Brit's mother. "We're spending two weeks in Alaska and Brit's staying with you."

"And twice," said Nannie, trembling, "I explained that I cannot take care of Brit. I have plans."

"You're eighty-six," muttered Brit's mother. "You don't have plans." And then, loud enough for Nannie to hear, she shouted, "You won't be taking care of Brit! Brit will be taking care of you!"

Nannie glared at her grown-up daughter. "Just go, then," she said, shooing Brit's parents back into their car. "Hurry up and leave."

2

Mom and Dad had a plane to catch, so they went. The moment they were out of sight, Nannie—who hardly ever cared what time it was—checked her watch.

Into the driveway whipped a metallic bronze GMC Safari van, spraying puddle water on Brit. Right behind it sped a black Saturn. Out of the Safari climbed an overweight guy in an ugly brown uniform. Nannie stepped forward like a contestant in a game show. "I'm Mrs. Scott!"

"And here's your car, ma'am," he said, handing her the keys.

Nannie had bought a car to replace her Caddy! No wonder she was tense; Mom would return this van to the dealership in two seconds. And no wonder Nannie forgot about the Alaska trip. Who cared where anybody else was going when Nannie was about to get her freedom back?

Brit had been there when Mom said to Nannie, "Your eyes are so bad you can't tell the difference between a trash barrel and a two-year-old at the side of the road. Your knees are so stiff it takes you five minutes to brake. You have to stop driving." Mom went right into Nannie's purse, fished out her driver's license, cut it in half and tossed it in the garbage. In vain, Nannie pleaded, "Without a car all I can do is gather dust and stare out the window." Because Nannie's house was three miles from a quart of milk, a committee meeting or a bridge game.

"I've hired an aide," said Brit's mother briskly. "She'll take you where you want to go. You won't even notice not having a car."

How could you not notice that you didn't have a car? Brit had been noticing that one all her life. She noticed every single kid who got their own car and every single one who didn't.

In spite of the rain, the dealer flung open every door to display the Safari's interior. Brit thought of a Safari as a jumped-up

3

utility van, but this model was deluxe: four leather bucket seats and a bench in back, cup holders everywhere, reading lights and possibly even a good sound system. Brit was very encouraged by how the first day of vacation was shaping up. Cars were everything.

Brit's parents commuted into New York City by train. Their dented and scratched Honda Accord had 110,000 miles on it, collected 5 miles at a time going back and forth from the train station. They had no plans for a new car. Only Brit wanted a decent car. And now Nannie, of all people, had one. (Well, as far as a midsized van could be decent. Personally Brit had her eye on a Mini Cooper in yellow. This was because of her lifelong crush on a boy actually named Cooper. Cooper no longer spoke to her or associated with her, but Brit liked to pretend that a Mini Cooper would give her that relaxed casual aura of car ownership, and then she could easily invite him for a drive, and it wouldn't seem pushy or date-ish, because the car was named for him.)

"Usually you'd have to drive me back to the lot, Mrs. Scott," said the guy, "but we're delivering the black Saturn this morning too, so I'll go on in that car. All you have to do is sign off."

Nannie wrote her name on a clipboard, which struck Brit as an odd way to buy a car.

"How about you hop into the driver's seat, Mrs. Scott, while I show you a few things?" said the guy.

Nannie had not "hopped" into or out of anything in years. Nannie's big skill was lowering. And she couldn't lower herself onto anything *really* low, because then she couldn't get up again. These days Nannie was always getting stuck on a sofa that was too soft or too deep.

The driver's side had a narrow running board, a step above

that, and handles. But even so, Brit didn't think her tiny little grandmother could get in without a boost. Why had Nannie bought this big box of a car? What did she want with extra seating and lots of luggage room? And how could she expect to get away with it once Mom was back?

"I don't require instruction, thank you," said Nannie. "I've been driving for three-quarters of a century."

The dealer was aghast. Could anybody that ancient still drive? He narrowed his eyes at Brit. "You're not letting this kid drive, are you?" he said sternly to Nannie. "You gotta be twenty-five years old to drive a rental car. You don't wanna break that law, Mrs. Scott. I can't leave the car with you, I think you're gonna let a kid drive."

A *rental* car? Brit thought.

"It has been delightful meeting you," said Nannie, "but I must go. Good morning."

The guy laughed, saluted her and leaped into the Saturn, which shot out the driveway Nannie-style. One thing Nannie had always done well was back up. She took a sight line in that rearview mirror and shot out into the road. Nannie and Grandpa had bought the house more than fifty years ago and there was probably fifty times more traffic now. Mom took away Nannie's driver's license precisely because Nannie backed into traffic without looking.

Nannie stroked the Safari as if patting somebody's new great-grandchild. She circled the vehicle, shutting each door the guy had left open. The doors made heavy satisfying slams. It wasn't just some tuna fish can of a car, but nice and solid. Still, no matter how solid the vehicle, Brit couldn't let Nannie drive. "Nannie," she said, "you can't drive without a license."

Nannie beamed. She opened her handbag. She liked purses a foot deep, six inches wide, and a foot and a half long. She carried paperbacks and lists and receipts and tissues and a hairbrush and lipsticks and basically anything small that looked as if it needed a place to live. Her wallet rose to the surface. Nannie did not have to open the wallet, since it was always open. Out spurted a license.

"Last week," Nannie said smugly, "I had a new aide who didn't know that Gail had destroyed my license. I had the aide drive me to the motor vehicle bureau, where I explained that I had mislaid it. They kindly made me another." Nannie threw her purse and umbrella into the Safari and reached for the lowest support handle. It was beyond her fingertips.

Clinging to the door and scrabbling at the seat, she got her right foot onto the lower step. Brit moved in close so she could make a save. Gripping the seat belt as Tarzan gripped vines, Nannie tried to haul herself in. The seat belt just lengthened. Nannie straightened her curved spine, got a fingerhold on the handle and, with great effort, placed her toes on the running board. Gasping for breath, she reached farther in, gripped a more distant handle, made it to the second step and fell over onto the seat. A minute later, she recovered enough to pull herself into an upright position. She was too short to see over the dashboard.

"Where are you headed?" asked Brit, knowing she must not let Nannie go anywhere, especially when Nannie had no view of the road.

Nannie lifted her chin. "Reunion."

And Brit knew that her grandmother did not see the driveway nor hear the rain. She saw her beloved college campus in

Maine as it had been in the fall of her freshman year, when four girls shared a suite in a brand-new dormitory called Buttermere.

Nannie Rawlings.

Florence Mirsky.

Aurelia Alan.

Daisy Ferrer.

Every single June since their college graduation, Nannie and "the girls" had gone to Reunion. Getting married (everybody), having babies (everybody), teaching Latin (Nannie), founding a museum (Aurelia), running an inn (Daisy), chairing boards (Florence), burying husbands (everybody)—nothing stood in their way. Then, last June, all four of the girls were told by their adult children, "You can't go this year. You're too old and sick." What their children didn't say—but Nannie certainly said to Brit—was "And we're not interrupting our interesting lives just to take you."

"Last year they won," said Nannie. "This year, they lose. This is our sixty-fifth reunion and we are not going to miss it. I'm the driver."

Brit saw the plan Nannie had hatched: *You won't let me drive? Fine. I'll get another license. You sold my car? Fine. I'll rent one.*

Nannie started the engine. It had a deep powerful purr, the sound of a van actually ready to go on a safari. Nannie, however, was too short to reach the pedals. "Britsy, kindly adjust the seat for me," said her grandmother.

"Okay," said Brit. "Shove over."

But Nannie was way beyond the age at which she could "shove over." Brit had to get in on the far side, crouch between the front seats, lift Nannie into the passenger seat, get behind the wheel, move the seat as low as it would go (Nannie would have a great view of the speedometer) and finally stick Nannie back behind the wheel. Her grandmother was as tiny as a five-year-old. If she ever got going, it would be one of those cases where the car seemed to be driving itself, out for a spin on a rainy day, cleverly managing its own turn signals.

Nannie's foot was still half an inch from the accelerator. Nannie never swore or used vulgar words and even now was probably not tempted. She just said, "Please go into the house, Britsy, and bring me two pillows."

Brit went into the house and got two pillows. On the way, she pulled her cell phone out of her jeans pocket and checked her messages. According to every text message she'd gotten so far this summer vacation (this was day one, and still pretty early in the morning, but even so Brit had heard from four girlfriends), everybody else was already bored and looking for something to do. I have something to do, thought Brit, and I don't know how to do it: stopping Nannie.

She quick called Hayley and explained, and Hayley, who always had the answer, said, "Just hire a driver. Enough money rents anything—look how they delivered Nannie's van right to her front door. The driver can pick up all those old ladies and take them to their reunion, and meanwhile, you stay with me! It'll be perfect! I'll tell my mother you're coming. Vacation is totally looking up."

Brit had always known that her best friend was brilliant. She got back into the van, and explained Plan B to Nannie.

But her grandmother took the pillows out of Brit's hands and wedged them behind her back. "Don't you interfere, young lady. I have no choice and I have to bring you to my reunion. But don't you forget—the way your *mother* forgets—that *I* am the grown-up and *you* are the child." Nannie struggled with her seat belt. In strange cars, Nannie could never find the slot for the tip to slide into. Brit clicked the belt in for her.

Nannie put the van in reverse. The Safari was automatic, so even though she wasn't touching the gas, it began moving slowly on its own. Since it was facing the house, it was now going backward toward the road. "There's a tree in the way," Brit mentioned. "Kind of a big one."

Nannie practically stood up on the floor to brake. The Safari lurched to a halt. Nannie shoved it into drive and now the van crept forward, relentlessly approaching the front steps. With all her strength (the strength a canary might have), Nannie yanked at the wheel, and because of excellent power steering, an actual collision with her house was avoided. The Safari slaughtered the rosebushes, accomplished a full circle and headed for the road again.

Brit stalled for time. "Aren't you taking a suitcase, Nannie?"

"Thank goodness you remembered! I have so much to bring. I made peanut brittle for Aurelia—she loves that. And maca- roons for Daisy; she loves those. And my best chocolate pound cake for Flo." Nannie braked. But the pressure of one toe was not enough to stop the Safari. And she didn't have the strength, a second time, to stand up on the pedal. Tugging at the wheel, Nannie thrust her little mauve shoe at anything on the floor. There was not time for Brit to slide her grandmother out of the driver's seat and take over before they ended up in the middle of traffic and got smashed to death, not an optimal first day of vacation. On the other hand, if Brit just jammed her dirty white sneaker on the brake, she'd crush Nannie's toes.

Brit grabbed the steering wheel and hauled it toward herself.

At the same moment, Nannie located the accelerator. The sudden spurt of gas spun the van through half the hedge and the rest of the flowers and dug tire ditches in the soft green grass. They both screamed. Nannie pressed harder on the floor. They crushed the herb garden, and the pillars of the front porch loomed in front of them. Brit kicked Nannie's foot off the accelerator, jabbed her left foot over and braked. They stopped with enough force to get whiplash. Brit put the car into park. The yard looked as if an entire football team's worth of vandals had been at work all night.

Nannie slumped against the pillows. Tears slid down the pale cheeks, which had never, not once, stayed out too long in the sun.

Brit's grandmother was so old she had only one daydream left—Reunion—and it was wrecked. Brit couldn't stand it. "Nannie, we can still go. I'll find a driver through the Yellow Pages and pay him anything to come right now. You'll have your sixty-fifth reunion. Everything will be all right."

"It won't be all right. We can't hire a driver. Nobody would go along with my plans. Oh, Britsy! Aurelia is counting on me and I'm going to let her down."

"What were your plans, Nannie?" said Brit as she texted Hayley. Plan B is out, she wrote. Think up Plan C.

"Aurelia's dreadful wicked son believes that since he's going to inherit her money anyway, he ought to be able to spend it right now, and Aurelia should just get out of his way and die. But she isn't dying, so he managed the next best thing. He visited her on a Sunday last November, and she was so pleased, because he rarely has time for her. He even took her to church, but after church, he didn't take her home. He threw her into an Alzheimer's facility."

Brit knew all about this. "Mom and Dad think it was for the

best, Nannie. Aurelia hasn't been well in years and she's on about a hundred medications and she couldn't take care of her house or get up and down the stairs. Her son loves her, Nannie; that's why he moved her closer to him."

"He does not love her! He loves her money. She's bought him off every year for fifty-nine years, and now he wants *all* the money. He's not a good child."

Whenever Nannie talked about "the girls," she also talked about their "children"—as if a guy fifty-nine years old could be called a child.

"He convinced the doctors—or paid them off, more likely!—that Aurelia has to be kept in a supervised ward. Then he put himself in charge of her. Aurelia does not have access to her own money! Well, she doesn't have Alzheimer's! Aurelia and I write frequently. Aurelia has all her marbles."

There was no finer compliment Nannie could give than to say that a person still had all her marbles.

The great fear of anybody eighty-six years old was indeed Alzheimer's disease. To misplace keys, forget a friend's name or not be able to figure out an easy crossword clue—it meant your mind was being eaten away; you were losing your marbles. Brit had never owned a marble, never seen anybody play marbles, didn't know what marbles had to do with brain cells. But Nannie fretted constantly about her marbles. "Losing them," she would whisper grimly when she could not find the fourth library book.

"Nannie, I can never find my library books either," Brit would say. "It has nothing to do with marbles and everything to do with being sloppy. You're eighty-six. You're never going to be a good housekeeper, so give it up. Library books are always going to be missing and they'll always surface eventually. Your marbles are fine."

Now Nannie turned her blue eyes to Brit. Every year those eyes faded a little. She looked terribly old. "I thought of everything!" cried Nannie. "I canceled my aides. I stopped the mail. The papers are being held. Today I plan to drive to Long Island to get Flo. Flo and I drive to Massachusetts and locate the nursing home. We remove Aurelia from her prison. To get her out of there, we may have to claim that we are her sisters. Nobody can argue with a sister, especially if they are wearing sensible shoes and have their hair done. We pretend we're merely going to lunch. Aurelia uses a walker and she's slow, but that is not a great impediment. We drive away. They suspect nothing."

Brit could see that a driver hired from the Yellow Pages might not cooperate in the snatching of an eighty-six-year-old woman with a walker.

"Then," finished Nannie triumphantly, "we confer with Aurelia's attorney and witness the new will she is writing, in which she leaves everything to the college instead of her dreadful son. We swing north, pick up Daisy and proceed to Reunion."

"I thought on a rainy day like this, you might teach me how to knit," said Brit. "But no, you want to pull off a kidnapping." Nannie would be the oldest living kidnapper in America. The Safari was her getaway car.

Nannie didn't hear Brit because she had forgotten to put her ears in. (Nannie never called them hearing aids because she hated the whole concept of needing aid.) "Daisy will never forgive us for not including her in the kidnapping," she said, "but we're eighty-six, so how many more years will we be alive to listen to Daisy complain? It's not our fault Daisy lives too far north to be part of the action."

Brit's phone rang, presumably with Hayley's Plan C.

But Nannie, not hearing the ring, took Brit's hand. "Britsy, I am a law-abiding person. But that's so yesterday." (Nannie adored slang and generally got it wrong; this time was perfect. Brit gave her a thumbs-up.) "Buttermeres," said Nannie, for she was even prouder of her dorm than of her college or her degree, "never surrender. Aurelia has lost all freedom and dignity and she is counting on me to restore them to her. I will not surrender to circumstance. It's time to break the rules."

Brit wasn't sure just how Nannie planned to break the rules, since she couldn't even get the Safari out of the driveway. "You're not tall enough to drive this car, Nannie."

"You are."

"It isn't legal for me to drive, Nannie. You heard the guy—if we have an accident, we're both in trouble. Police trouble . . . insurance company trouble . . . rental car company trouble." Brit didn't bother to mention Mom trouble, which was the biggie in their family.

"Then don't have an accident. Don't worry," said the grandmother who could not see the road or read the signs, "I'll navigate. You'll steer. Load the car, Brit. Then we hit the parkway. We have a kidnap scheduled."

CHAPTER 2

Nannie had packed one suitcase for cold weather (Maine could be frigid even in June) and one for warm weather (a person could hope). She had car blankets, bottled water, dented old aluminum beach chairs, tissues and a cardboard box filled with road maps from Grandpa's early driving years. Nannie powdered her nose (Nannie never went to the bathroom; she powdered her nose) while Brit stashed all this in the van. Brit solved the problem of the van's height by bringing out Nannie's one-step kitchen stool.

Nannie mounted the stool with delight, slid into her bucket seat and put on her cataract sunglasses—plastic goggles with inch-wide side bars. So little of Nannie showed between her hair and her chin that if you hadn't believed in aliens from distant planets before, you would now.

Brit stowed the step stool in the van, got in the driver's seat, tossed her backpack on top of Nannie's purse and umbrella and turned on the engine. She adjusted the mirrors, located the windshield wipers, raised the seat, turned north and headed for the Merritt Parkway. Her parents did not allow her to do any highway driving. Mom would be furious.

But she won't find out, thought Brit, and since when do kidnappers worry about what their mothers think?

She remembered suddenly that she had a phone message waiting. She could not figure out how to retrieve it while driving. Entrance ramps to the Merritt Parkway were short and difficult. Even seasoned drivers cringed when they had to get on the Merritt. Kidnappers don't cringe, so Brit took a quick glance at oncoming traffic and slammed the accelerator down. The Safari hurtled forward. In moments she was going faster than anybody and had passed several little sedans.

"First we get Flo," said Nannie excitedly.

Brit lived about thirty-five miles east of New York City. Flo also lived east of New York City, but out on Long Island, so she was parallel to them, except with a finger of Atlantic Ocean in between. They'd speed down the Merritt, swing left on some bridge and scoot out on Long Island, having made a huge U-turn. Piece of cake.

Her cell phone rang.

Brit had her phone programmed to warn her when it was Mom; everybody had their mother on a special ring, because that call you had to answer. Mostly mothers had one question—where r u?—and if you didn't snatch up that phone and answer, you were dead and your parents might even take away your phone, which was just like being dead. For her mother's ring, Brit had chosen the Beethoven's Fifth theme, that ominous one: dum dum dum daaaaah.

Brit thought fast. If she said, "Hi, Mom, have a relaxing flight to Alaska; Nannie and I will just be out kidnapping, mainly on interstates, in a rental car I'll be driving illegally," the response would not be positive.

Brit didn't use a purse. She stuffed anything she needed into her backpack or pockets. She twitched herself but didn't feel a phone resting in a pants pocket, so, leaning to her right, she kept the wheel steady with her left hand and fished around the inside of her backpack with her right hand, at sixty-five miles per hour while passing. I'm an awesome driver, she thought, feeling the little oblong of her beloved cell phone.

Then she noticed she was actually going eighty-seven and was about to drive into the trunk of the car in front of her.

Brit jerked her foot off the accelerator, found the brake, braked too hard and was down to forty so fast that the car behind her almost rear-ended them. He honked furiously and Brit discovered that when reaching to her right for the phone, she had pulled the wheel in the same direction and was now within an inch of the trees that bordered the Parkway. Holding the phone in her teeth, she straightened the van, got her speed back to sixty-five, avoided meeting the eye of the guy behind her, who was now passing because she was obviously insane and incompetent, and then said breezily into her saliva-dampened phone, "Hi, Mom."

Uh-oh, she thought. I don't have my headset because I didn't think I'd be driving. It's illegal to talk on the phone if you have to take your hands off the wheel.

16

"Hi, honey. It's been an easy drive to the airport. No traffic whatsoever on the Merritt."

Brit didn't know what Merritt Parkway Mom was driving on, because Brit, right behind her (they were going the same way, except Mom would turn off at the airport), had never seen such heavy traffic in her life. "That's good, Mom."

"Is Nannie calming down?"

Nannie in fact was leaning forward like a setter pointing toward a rabbit. She could see the future and it was Reunion.

"She's fine," said Brit, struggling to drive in heavy traffic on narrow lanes, going sixty-five, holding a phone and telling lies. She saw with dismay the orange cones of construction ahead. Her lane was about to narrow into a thread. Brit liked lots of room on both sides of a car. I can't fit there! she thought.

She and her mother often called each other two, three or four times a day. They had a record of nine calls in one day, when Brit and Hayley were at the mall and kept needing permission to buy more. Mom was probably planning to narrate the whole Alaska trip by phone. Brit needed to put a stop to that right now. "We're going shopping, Mom," she improvised. "You know how Nannie hates it when other people's phones ring in stores, so I'm turning mine off for a while."

"How are you getting to the mall?" asked Mom, quite reasonably, since as far as she knew, they had no car.

"The aide got here early," Brit lied.

"Darling, the mall isn't open yet."

"We're getting coffee first," said Brit wildly, forgetting that she herself didn't drink coffee and Nannie sipped her one cup at five a.m.

"Clearly Nannie is giving you a difficult time, Britsy. That is unfair. Let me speak to Nannie now."

Brit hated being called Britsy, except by Nannie, and even then she wanted Nannie to stop. "Nannie and I want jelly doughnuts, though, and that means the coffee shop. Don't worry about us, Mom, just have a good time." The phone slipped. When she tried to reposition it, she lost her grip on the wheel and headed once more in the direction of the trees. This time there were no trees; there was a concrete bridge abutment. Brit corrected her steering. She corrected too far and nearly took out the passenger door of a very small, almost invisible car on her left.

She was beginning to see why there was a headset law.

"You're such a good girl," said Mom fondly.

"Have a safe flight!" Brit yelled, and she shut down her cell phone, dropped it to the floor and concentrated on keeping the Safari between dotted lines.

"What did she say?" asked Nannie.

"That I'm a good girl."

"No, you're not," said Nannie happily. "You're a co-conspirator, saving Aurelia and restoring her freedom and helping her give the money to a deserving heir."

Brit wondered how much money this was.

One thing about the girls: they'd bought their houses in lovely neighborhoods many years ago. The houses alone made them millionaires. Plus, if they were like Nannie, they'd been thrifty and spent nothing. Nannie still wore the first bibbed apron she bought at a church fair back before she even got married. And when the girls (or their husbands, when they were alive) invested money, they didn't do it in risky tech stocks. The girls probably hadn't lost much in the recent scary stock market. So when Aurelia's son wanted all the money, there could be an awful lot of money to want.

Brit was about to be the instrument of his downfall. Too bad

Nannie had rented this utility van. A better getaway car would be a Corvette, although hard to fit four old ladies and their aluminum beach chairs into. She still wanted a Mini Cooper most. Probably because she still wanted Coop most.

Coop suffered because of a difficult older brother. Rupert (perhaps the name Rupert would make anybody lash out) had been a lifelong source of trouble. If Rupert wasn't taking his father's Mercedes without permission and going ninety-seven in a thirty-five-mile zone, he was keying the vice principal's car or starting a fight at the hockey rink, which ended in bloody noses all around, or filching his aunt's credit card to get himself a decent DVD player. Rupert never hurt anybody (except at games or if you were a referee) and he seemed to steal only from close family members, but he left a memorable trail.

Coop therefore was the most supervised teenage boy in Connecticut because his parents weren't about to have a *second* Rupert. So Coop was denied a driver's license and never allowed anywhere without his parents' consent. It wouldn't surprise Brit if Coop's parents had installed tracking devices in his shoes. Probably when they got suspicious, they made him photograph his surroundings on his camera phone, so they could verify his position. Rupert meanwhile went to college in Montana, where everybody hoped he would stay, adding to Montana's problems but making life ever so much easier here in Connecticut.

The rental guys had set the car radio for KISS-FM. Brit sang along. But Nannie, who never listened to the radio, and certainly not to pop, began fiddling with it. "Ten-Ten-Wins, Brit," she said. "They give traffic reports and what bridges to avoid." Nannie turned the volume up higher than drug dealers played rap. The car shuddered with news about roads Brit had never heard of. The Major Deegan was backed up twenty-five minutes. The George Washington Bridge had forty-minute delays. The L.I.E., whatever that was, was the worst in living memory.

"What exactly is our route to Flo's?" Brit yelled over the din of the radio.

Nannie, of course, heard only a fraction of what Brit had said. "Isn't Flo a nice nickname?" she said. "I love nicknames, except for the name I'm stuck with. Nannie might be acceptable if it were short for Nancy or Anne, and I could have discarded it when I grew up, but it's my real name. I always wanted to be Irene or Winifred. And even though lots of dear children call their grandmothers Nannie, it's odd to have my granddaughter address me by my first name."

In Brit's class of 407, 11 were named Brittany. The other 10 had all done something to stand out, so each of them was "the Brittany who . . ."—but she personally was better at blending than shining. Still, even in her worst moments, Brit had never wished to be named Winifred.

In a moment of bravado, Brit had moved out of the safe, easy right-hand lane and taken up a position in the left. The Safari was so high and wide that Brit now had no view of the right lane, and it turned out that the whole let's-not-have-an-accident thing depended on seeing who was coming from behind in the right lane. She adjusted the side mirror and the rearview mirror but couldn't get oriented to the reflections.

"You see," said Nannie, "Flo had lots of money, which was so exciting. The rest of us were comfortable, but Flo was the real thing: rich. She was Jewish," said Nannie, for whom it was now early September, sixty-nine years ago. "I had never met a Jew. My parents wanted me to move out of Buttermere."

Brit stared at her grandmother, a poor choice because her hands followed her eyes, the wheel turned toward the right again and a horn sounded so viciously that Brit expected to be turned into hamburger on the spot. She jerked back into her lane.

"But she wasn't a practicing Jew," said Nannie, "and I was so disappointed, because I thought we would have seders and perhaps sing minor-key hymns in temples. Instead, she came with me one night to Christian Fellowship and then of course *her* parents wanted *her* to move out, away from the dread influence of Nannie Rawlings."

"*You* were a bad influence?"

Nannie nodded proudly. "Flo introduced me to wine. I had no idea people actually consumed it. I, on the other hand, introduced Flo to Christmas decorations. You should see the tree she has every year."

But since Flo had not moved out of Buttermere, Brit assumed that the Mirskys came for a visit, looked at Nannie, yawned and shrugged.

"Flo always had grand ideas at crazy hours and she could talk Daisy and me into anything. Not Aurelia, of course. Aurelia would never agree to jimmy open the kitchen window and break in after midnight to make sandwiches. It's so exciting to think that even at eighty-six you can be a new person. Aurelia wouldn't snitch a bread crust and now she's designed her own kidnapping."

"*You* jimmied a window, Nannie?"

"Of course not. Flo jimmied it. I was a bystander."

"That's so yesterday, Nannie. If there's one thing kidnappers aren't, it's bystanders."

They left Connecticut and crossed into New York State. Large road signs began mentioning various bridges, interstates and exits that were coming up. "Which bridge, Nannie?"

"Throgs Neck."

Brit believed this name only because she saw it on a sign. "Is there a toll, Nannie? Do you have cash ready?"

"I have E–ZPass."

"That was your Caddy. This is a rental car."

"Oh, my," said Nannie. "I forgot to bring any cash."

This necessitated getting off the highway someplace in Westchester County and scouring the neighborhood for an ATM. Brit didn't care whether the neighborhood was crime ridden or full of millionaires, and she didn't care whether they found Citibank or Fleet. She just didn't want to back up or parallel park. The fourth ATM she spotted fit the requirement. "I'll get the money, Nannie. Give me your card. What's your PIN number?"

Nannie tried to remember her PIN.

"Or," threatened Brit, "we drive all the way home, go to your regular bank, cash a check and start over."

"We can't do that. We have a boat to catch."

Poor Nannie was getting her nouns mixed up. The transportation style they were using was definitely not a boat.

"Three-two-two-one," Nannie remembered joyfully. "Get two hundred dollars."

Brit tapped in 3221 and then did the kind of thing her mother did—invaded Nannie's personal affairs. She did not hit Fast Cash but went into Nannie's account to make sure they could afford this. Nannie's balance was four thousand dollars, which ought to cover tolls between here and Flo's. Brit loved starting a vacation with four thousand dollars. She gave the two hundred in twenties to Nannie, who let them sift down in the general direction of her purse. Brit gathered them up, stuck nine in her backpack and kept one for the toll.

Her merge back onto the parkway was brilliant. Pride lasted sixty seconds and then the cars-only parkway merged with an interstate, and a million trucks elbowed into her lane. Cement barriers raised their vicious teeth inches from the side of the Safari. Cars rocketed into traffic from both sides. Signs leaped up from their stalks, flung themselves at Brit's eyes and vanished before they could be read.

Brit couldn't even tell what road she was on. It might be I-95, but it also might be I-295. And now there seemed to be I-695 as well. Throgs Neck Bridge seemed to require two of these. How could she drive on two roads at once? And what *was* a throg, and what did its neck look like?

"Let's sing to pass the time," said Nannie, turning off the radio. "There was so much singing then, Brit. We all sang. Patriotic songs, sacred songs, Broadway hits and folk songs."

The road kept splitting, lanes peeling away, and the signs that named these splits came *after* the turns, so you couldn't possibly know what to do until it was too late, and even if you did know, all the zooming cars made your move impossible or fatal. How could Nannie think that Brit had enough experience for this road? How could New York State even claim it *was* a road? It was a construction zone and a torture chamber and a homicide district—but a road?

"*She'll be comin' round the mountain when she comes,*" Nannie started.

Brit knew the song. Each verse repeated one sentence five times, presumably so the mentally impaired could chime in toward the end.

She'll be comin' round the mountain when she comes,
She'll be comin' round the mountain,

She'll be comin' round the mountain,
She'll be comin' round the mountain when she comes.

Brit was still in the left lane when she realized that the bridge required a right-hand exit. She checked her side mirror. The right lane looked nice and empty, so she pulled into it. It was not empty. A gasoline tanker was barreling from behind to fill the slot. Its horn screamed, its brakes shrieked and Brit thought, We're dead. She'd be the centerpiece of one of those ghastly teen funerals, where everybody sobs, "How we loved her! She had such potential!"

Brit shoved the accelerator to the floor, flew across the lane and made it out the exit, holding the wheel so tightly her fingers hurt. She shook them back into hand shapes.

Nannie, who had noticed nothing, finished the second verse—*She'll be riding six white horses when she comes*—and moved on to the third: *Oh, we'll all go out to meet her when she comes.* "I've always wondered who she is," said Nannie thoughtfully. "I think of her in the mountains. West Virginia, maybe."

Brit reached the tolls. There must have been twenty booths. She had to cross in front of half of them to get in a cash lane. She wasn't sobbing, but only because she didn't have time.

On the left side of the tollbooths was a police car. On the right side was another police car. Up on the high arch of the bridge, she spotted a third. There had probably been some sort of terror warning, and New York was in a state of high alert, and she, Brittany Anne Bowman, illegal driver, was about to mow down a tollbooth.

Trucks herded into her slot, her change was given back in a nanosecond, and then she and a million other vehicles were ripping over the bridge, which had lanes even narrower than the Merritt under construction. Furthermore, if she made a mistake, there was water to fall into.

"See the skyline!" cried Nannie, taking off her cataract goggles to let in more light. "New York City is so beautiful! No one could ever tire of New York! Brit, honey, are you admiring the view?"

Brit's view was the back of a filthy graffiti-painted truck that was spewing fumes and little pellets all over her windshield. "Nannie!" she yelled. "Read the signs! Tell me what to do! Do we want the Cross Island Parkway? Two-ninety-five? Four-ninety-five? The Van Wyck? The L.I.E.? The Long Island Expressway?"

"Those two are the same road."

"But do we want them?" Brit shrieked.

Signs for Kennedy Airport appeared. She imagined catching up to Mom and Dad, such a horrifying thought that she examined the traffic for dented Hondas, and now every single car seemed to be an old black sedan.

"Take the L.I.E.," said Nannie.

This was good because the L.I.E. was not the route to Kennedy Airport, but bad because the L.I.E. had exits and entrances every few feet. Cars leaped in and out of Brit's lane like cats at play. Brit was sweating as if she were playing tournament tennis. Not that she had ever been in a tournament. Brit preferred spectator sports and only played sports in high school because her friends did. It was difficult to believe she was now voluntarily participating in a Long Island sport in which death and dismemberment were the penalties.

Brit's phone rang. Impossible. She had turned it off. Had she been so flustered after lying to Mom that she hadn't even been able to push buttons? Even more impossible, Nannie heard it and picked it up.

"Don't answer it yet!" yelled Brit. "First see who it is!"

"How do I do that?"

"Read the words," suggested Brit.

"It says Lindsay Dorrelle," Nannie reported.

This was not good. Lindsay Dorrelle was Nannie's next-door neighbor. Lindsay checked on everything in Nannie's life. You were supposed to be grateful for neighbors like that, but Nannie wasn't.

Without warning, the L.I.E. ground to a halt. Brit jammed on the brake, came to a full stop, didn't get hit, didn't hit anybody else. She snatched the phone out of Nannie's hand. "Hi, Lindsay," she said sweetly.

I'm not actually driving, she told herself. This conversation is perfectly legal. Nevertheless, Brit hunched down behind the wheel and talked into her lap.

"Britsy, honey," said Lindsay affectionately.

Brit *really* hated being called Britsy by Lindsay Dorrelle. "What's up, Lindsay?"

"Honey, your grandmother is missing. I can't find her. And her entire yard has been vandalized. I've called the police and they're here now, trying to establish your poor dear grandmother's whereabouts. Try not to be afraid. Sometimes these things turn out to be misunderstandings." Her voice implied that usually these things turned out to be mass murder.

The traffic took off. Motorcycles and trucks and trailers and pickups and Beemers and Volkswagens and Audis and Fords and boats being towed made up for lost time. Brit raced helplessly in their midst. "Everything's fine, Lindsay!" she screamed. "Nannie's with me! I'll call you back in five minutes!" She threw the phone on the floor and gripped the wheel. She took the first exit and that didn't work; it was another highway. She took the first exit off that, and that didn't work; it was a sort of divided local highway. She pulled into the first driveway and that worked fine; it was some little strip mall with a bank and a dry cleaner and a restaurant. That was good, because probably Brit would never find the courage to get back on the L.I.E. and they'd have to live here, and at least they could get money and keep their clothes clean and eat.

"I need to powder my nose in that little restaurant, Brit," said Nannie.

"In a minute." She picked up the phone and hit *69 and Lindsay answered in the voice of one eager to tattle. "Britsy, honey, it sounded as if you were in traffic."

"Nannie's at my house," she yelled, so that Nannie would hear and repeat the same lies. "We're watching TV. Everything's fine." She was pretty sure Lindsay wouldn't drive all the way to Brit's house to check, and even if she did, she didn't have a key and couldn't get in there and peek under the beds or anything.

"Well, her front yard certainly isn't fine. The police need to talk to you, Britsy, so they can get leads on the perpetrator."

Police? How could this be happening on the first morning of her summer vacation? If Brit explained that Nannie had done her own vandalizing, the police would want to know where the vandal car was now and whether this incompetent eighty-six-year-old was still driving it . . . but if Brit *didn't* tell, the police would start tracking down teenagers with a history of doing wheelies on the school lawn. Rupert was lucky to be in Montana.

"Officer Todd here," said the next voice.

"Hi," she gushed. "This is Brittany Anne Bowman. I'm so sorry Lindsay Dorrelle bothered you, Officer Todd. I'm just learning how to drive?" she said to him, in the questioning tone of a person with a lame excuse. "And I mowed down the rose garden? And panicked and dug tracks in the yard? But I'll fix it. I'll be in there with a shovel and grass seed before you know it." Great, she thought. I not only get held responsible, I have to spend all summer repairing grass.

"How old are you, Brittany Anne?" asked the cop.

Even though she'd introduced herself with both names, she also hated being called Brittany Anne. It made her sound like a kindergartner in a fluffy skirt asking for new crayons. "Sixteen. I've had my license only two weeks and I don't back up that well and it seemed logical to practice at Nannie's." She hoped Lindsay Dorrelle would not explain to the cop that Nannie did not possess a car to practice with.

"Uh-huh. Can I talk to your grandmother?"

Brit handed over the cell phone. Nannie had no cell phone of her own and regarded them, and most technology, with fear and loathing. "How does it work, Britsy?" she said anxiously. "What do I speak into?"

"I'm not going to dignify that with an answer. It's a phone. Hold it right side up and start talking."

Nannie giggled. "Yoo-hoo," she called to the policeman. "You are so sweet to follow up on this, Officer Todd. But of course it didn't happen on a public road, where it might actually be a police concern. So delightful chatting with you. Good-bye now."

Officer Todd did not give up quite that easily, but when at last that ended, and Nannie won, and when they got to the restaurant, and Nannie had powdered her nose, and the hostess wanted to take them to a table, and Nannie said they really didn't have time, and the hostess looked a little dangerous, and they couldn't leave quickly because "quick" was no longer among Nannie's skills, and when Brit had Nannie re-established in the front seat with her seat belt snapped and was circling the entire strip mall to avoid backing up, she said, "And where exactly does Flo live, Nannie? Which exit off the L.I.E.?"

"Oh," said Nannie thoughtfully. "Where *does* Flo live?"

Brit wanted to text message everyone in her entire life. She would write *Aaaaaaaaaaaahh!* and they would understand.

"You see, Flody had two children," said Nannie, revealing yet another ghastly nickname for Florence. "Lenny and George. Lenny died in Vietnam. I don't know that Flody ever got over it. George married Danielle and they had three children, who must be in their thirties now, all with impressive careers. I think they're all on second marriages too. They rush all over the globe and get things done, but they only rush to Flo's at High Holidays. I've always thought it was such an asset to have High Holidays. It implies that you really must go home. In any event, Flo's husband died, dear Ralph, and Flo remarried, I forget his name, such a sweet boy, and then *he* died, and she married *again* and I really *will* have to think of *his* name, because of course it's *her* name too."

Brit got back on the divided local street, spotted the entrance to the connecting highway and, from there, got back on the L.I.E., all without flinching or sobbing. "In other words, we're going to get Flo, but we don't know where she lives or what her name is."

Nannie settled her cataract glasses over her eyes, enclosing herself in a dim and shadowy world. "Don't worry," said the grandmother who couldn't see *before* she put the cataract glasses on and now she *really* couldn't see, "I'll recognize the exit when we get there. Stay alert. I'll yell at the last second."

CHAPTER 3

The L.I.E. went on forever. They should have bumped into Canada by now. Maybe Ireland. Brit wanted to scream. She loved screaming, which was perfectly acceptable at basketball games, but not good during SATs or while driving with Nannie. So she didn't scream, even when Nannie sang the fourth verse of "She'll Be Comin' Round the Mountain," the one where they all have chicken and dumplings when she comes. Brit was feeling pretty experienced at highways now, so she flipped her cell phone open to check her calls. Communication always made her feel better.

Hayley had written, Plan C. Call on Coop. Have him save the day. He's the type.

As if Brit was going to call Coop. Just thinking about it gave her a headache.

A phone call took a certain amount of guts because your naked voice was hanging there. A text message was remote, as if anybody could have written it; it was just some electronic scribble.

Brit had fallen for Cooper James in seventh grade. The other boys still had the soft smooth cheeks of children, but Coop started to get a beard and had to shave daily. Brit would spend the entire language arts class wanting to touch Coop, who sat next to her. She would consider each separate body part, starting with that jaw, bristling like a man's, and moving outward and upward and downward. Their language arts teacher had a different view of facial hair: she said only thugs and dictators went around with shadows on their cheeks. "Where," said the teacher, smirking, "has our dear little Coopsy gone?" Brit, who that year was still being called Britsy, wanted to kill the teacher for Coop's sake. As for Coop himself, he was trapped. If he attacked the teacher, it would fulfill his parents' worst nightmare—they had another Rupert. If he didn't attack, every kid in school would feel free to pat his cheek and call him Coopsy.

He won a nationwide contest that year with his essay "Seventh Grade: The First Thousand Years." Brit had downloaded it from the school's Web site and still had it in a separate folder on her desktop, alongside "The First Thousand Years of My Crush on Coop." Every now and then she added a new document, such as "Our Wedding Invitation" or "Our Honeymoon Plans." Grow up, Hayley would tell her. Trash that stuff. But occasionally Brit had to reread it, because her electronic life plan worked out so well.

As time went on, Coop became keen on sports Brit found

upsetting (like boxing) or boring (like weight lifting) or were out of town (like ice hockey; their school had a team but not a rink), and so along with becoming hairier, Coop became larger, stronger and wider. He liked to wear T-shirts featuring skulls or spiders. The language arts teacher had been right; Cooper James looked like a thug. Brit totally loved that look.

This winter they had all been in the library doing research projects. Most people had taken a cube to use a school computer, but Brit was using her laptop. She left it on when she went off to paw through old magazines, and headed back to find Cooper James sitting in her seat, typing on her keyboard—staring at her screen. She knew in a moment that she was ruined, and she was right. Coop jumped away from that laptop as if it contained a curse that would destroy his entire life. He spotted her standing among the books, and stuck his finger down his throat, the universal sign for gagging. For the rest of junior year, he never sat near her, said a word to her or used her name. Kids in their class traveled in pairs and groups, and every-body was always texting each other to make plans. If Coop read that Brit was going to be in the group, he dropped out.

The only person who knew what had happened was Hayley.

"He's a computer genius," said Hayley, shrugging. "He proba-bly has this magnetic attraction to a fresh new computer like your laptop. His fingers just automatically open up secret files. At least now we know that when a boy finds out a girl has their honeymoon planned, all he wants to do is throw up."

Brit thought about that all winter and all spring: Cooper James thought of her and wanted to throw up.

Plan C. Call on Coop. Right.

Maybe by the time she and Cooper had *their* sixty-fifth

reunion, they could laugh about it. But not now. Anyway, Plan C had developed by itself and Brit was now driving really fast toward a person whose name they didn't know in a town they couldn't remember.

She checked the rest of her messages.

Molly had written, movies? Tish had written, No movies. Anything else. Thomas had written, yes movies.

They had texted. But there was also one voice message and the caller ID read: Cooper James.

Impossible. Somebody must have stolen his phone. Coop would never call her. But he had. What if—dream of dreams— Coop wanted Brit to go to the movies too and panicked at the last second and didn't leave his message after all and—

I'm on Long Island, thought Brit. Soon to go to Massachusetts. Then Maine. It could be a week before I'm back!

She was stunned. Her life was on hold. Her summer plans were not her own; she couldn't even *make* plans.

"Here we are!" cried Nannie, as excited as a child on her birthday. "This is our exit! Britsy, get off, get off!"

Brit had forgotten that she was driving. She had forgotten trucks and traffic and turn signals and cops. They could have had a fatal accident and she wouldn't have noticed until the metal edge of some truck penetrated her little brain.

"Turn north!" cried Nannie.

"Nannie, I don't know the difference between north and a hamburger."

"Left. Back toward Long Island Sound. We're going to Stony Brook." These days names and places slid from Nannie's mind like food from a plate, whereas verbs and old memories stood firm. Given time, the nouns usually wandered up to Nannie, like old friends she'd forgotten about until their Christmas letters came again that year.

The roads here were mellow compared to the highway, and yet much more difficult—with pedestrians and red lights and curves and dogs and people backing out of their driveways as fast as Nannie ever did. Brit had no time to listen to Coop's message.

Whatever he wanted her to do, she couldn't do it anyway, so she might as well wait until she had some privacy. Then, if it was good news, she could play his voice over and over, and if it was bad news, she could sob all alone.

Nannie remembered Flo's address. "Harbor Lane," she crowed joyfully. "Stony Brook is a village with darling little white clapboard buildings like farmhouses," Nannie told her, "but they're actually the bank and Talbots." Talbots was the perfect clothing store for Nannie, because it had a big line of boring petites. Brit often waited in Talbots while Nannie dithered between silk twin sets in avocado green or desert taupe.

"Flo moved here because when Ralph finished his post-doctoral studies he became a research scientist," said Nannie. Nannie never identified the people in her stories. She assumed that of course you knew who everybody was and why research scientists moved to Long Island. But there was a lot of repetition in Nannie's stories, so you always had a second chance at figuring out the players. "And then Ralph died. He was so young! I don't think he was fifty. Flo fell in love with whatever his name was. He didn't last long either. We hardly got to the wedding and we were showing up for the funeral. And then Arnie—that's her third husband—died a year ago."

Nannie always thought something had just happened and then, on further reflection, decided she was mistaken. Sure enough, Nannie said thoughtfully, "No, it must have been five years ago. Maybe ten."

Five *days* ago, maybe ten, Brit had been signing yearbooks. And Nannie was right; already it seemed remote. Twenty-four hours ago, she had been hugging classmates good-bye. People who had ignored her for months were suddenly sorry to part. Cooper James was not one of those. He could not be calling for details about an assignment; there weren't any over the summer, and for that kind of thing he'd text Anthony anyway.

Last week, Molly had insisted that Brit prepare something to write in Coop's yearbook.

"He doesn't like me," Brit had pointed out.

"Everybody likes you. You're one of those annoying completely likeable people. And I know he likes you because he watches you all the time," said Molly. "Sign his yearbook."

He watched Brit all the time so he could stay out of her way. "I bet he didn't even buy a yearbook," said Brit.

Coop, who planned to be a filmmaker and never moved without his camcorder, had wanted to do a video yearbook. To his astonishment, the whole school rose up against him. They wanted a regular old book of photos with their graduation year on the cover. The senior class organized against Cooper, voting 87 percent for tradition, while Coop's own junior class formed its yearbook committee a year early, to fend off any video assault planned by Cooper James.

"He's on the ice hockey team," Molly pointed out, "and High School Bowl, and he co-chaired the fund-raiser for the court-yard picnic tables. Of course he bought a yearbook! His picture has to be in it three times plus class photo. You've always adored him, Brit. Don't let this moment get away from you. Write something affectionate, meaningful and haunting."

Brit was sure Coop felt haunted by her already.

When the yearbooks were delivered, everybody leafed through, hoping to find some special picture of themselves, something beyond team photos—and on the candids page was a black-and-white photograph of Brit sitting alone on the picnic table that Coop had raised the funds for. Her sober face was lifted to a gray sky while snowflakes sifted down upon her cheeks. She looked profound and intelligent. "It doesn't look a bit like you," everybody told her, which Brit found rather offensive.

Still, everybody held their yearbooks open to that page and asked her to sign on top of it. She was thrilled when Cooper got in line with everybody else. He didn't say anything. He didn't look at her, just handed her his pen. She took it, warm from his hand. Remembering his essay, she wrote, *School won't last a thousand years after all, will it? One more year and we graduate. A yearbook is like autumn—leaves falling, and everybody going away.*

"He wants a signature, not an essay," said Anthony, looking over Coop's shoulder.

Love, Brit, she scribbled, and Coop looked as if he'd like to abandon his book now that it was contaminated by those two words, but he picked it up and was turning away, and she said, "Coop, please sign mine?" Trapped by Anthony, who graciously stepped back, Coop flipped through Brit's yearbook, circled himself in the hockey team photo and printed, *Best wishes. Cooper James.* Not the statement of a guy planning to phone her in a few days.

Brit couldn't take the suspense. Every blind curve forced her to drive more slowly, until finally she was driving at the same speed as any other little old lady on the road, creeping around nervously, hoping not to smash some toddler on a tricycle. A person going twenty miles an hour could listen to her phone. She checked Coop's message.

But there was only breathing. No words. The bum! How could he do this to her?

"Here we are!" Nannie indicated a driveway with an ankle-deep layer of tiny white pebbles. No house was in sight. The driveway looked like the kind that was narrow here, would be narrow for a long way and would have no turnaround space, and Brit would have to back up a quarter mile to get out.

Brit was past the point of no return when she thought of a question she should have asked earlier. "The name on the mailbox is Laurence, Nannie. Was Arnie's last name Laurence?"

"Oh, dear me, no. Heff. Arnie Heff. In many ways, I liked Arnie better than I liked Ralph or that second one, whoever he was. Arnie and Flo were terribly athletic, you know. They golfed and played tennis and sailed and Arnie was always training for a marathon and Flo was always swimming right in the ocean. Now, I would never swim in the actual water of the actual ocean. I hate snails and jellyfish."

"Nannie, are you telling me this is not Flo's house?"

"Correct," said Nannie. "You see, last year Flo fell off her bicycle and broke her right arm and wrist and the bones wouldn't mend and of course she's right-handed and so she couldn't drive or scramble eggs or play the violin or anything. She's better now, although she still isn't playing the violin, and of course the violin was her great joy in life. But she has strength in *one* hand, which is enough to drive *locally,* although not to Maine, but that's why George and Danielle said she couldn't go to the reunion, and they took away *her* car and license, just the way Gail—"

"So where does Flo live?" screamed Brit, driving helplessly

toward some family named Laurence, and she hated them already, because they were the kind of people who could back up, and she wasn't feeling very kindly toward Nannie either.

"Brit, I have told you and told you how rude it is to shout."

Brit swallowed some things she would like to shout at her grandmother. "I'm sorry, Nannie. Where might Flo be residing at this actual moment in time?"

"George and Danielle wanted her to move into Sunrise Assisted Living after the accident and Flo said she'd sail off on an iceberg before she moved into an institution with special facilities for the memory impaired, so they compromised on a retirement center, the kind where you have your own apartment but they serve three meals a day in an elegant dining room." Nannie frowned. "I wonder how to get there."

The driveway came out at a large contemporary home with windows that had a world-class view of water, harbor and sky. Brit didn't care about views, just turn space. There was plenty of it. In fact, there was a lot of land, period. Brit didn't know what land was worth on Long Island, but the same land straight across the water in Connecticut would be worth millions.

"Thirty-two acres," Nannie told her, and Brit upped her estimate. "This was Arnie's," said Nannie. "He left it to Flo, and Flo was supposed to leave it to a land trust, which would tear the house down, and the land would revert to the wild. Well! Didn't George and Danielle whip out a plan for subdividing the property." Nannie sniffed, which she often did at a point where Brit's classmates would use a four-letter word.

"Flo had to act. She couldn't wait until she was dead, you see. Last month, Flo deeded all this to the land trust. These Laurence people are renting. When their lease is up, the house comes down."

"Wow," said Brit. "George and Danielle could have had a zillion dollars just by finding a builder? Bet they're ticked."

"Indeed," said Nannie. "The point is, however, that Flo's decision gave Aurelia courage. That's how we reached the kidnap plan. You cannot let your sons run your life. Flo's son George actually took it very nicely, but Aurelia's son will be furious. He could also be dangerous. I've always wondered if Aurelia is physically afraid of him."

He's fifty-nine, thought Brit. Way too old to do anything.

It dawned on her that if Flo's and Aurelia's houses were worth a ton of money, so was Nannie's. Perhaps Nannie was also changing her will and leaving the house to a good cause. Brit would have said she personally wasn't greedy and didn't care about money or land. But her heart sank. Not have Nannie's house one day? Not have her own little girl sleep in the same bedroom where first her mother and then Brit slept? Not have Nannie's china and silver set at the same old table?

Nannie had volunteered at Hospice for years. If Nannie was leaving everything to Hospice, Brit would have to say, "Oh, Nannie, I love when dying strangers get it all and living granddaughters get nothing."

Right away, Brit knew she would have a terrible attitude. "Are you changing your will too?" she asked casually. She imagined Mom and Dad at the rail of their cruise ship, scouring the horizon for whales, while Nannie was busily cutting them out of her will.

"Darling, I have no money to leave. Your father and mother support me. I'm sure they wish *I* would move into a retirement center too, so they could sell my house and pay my expenses out of that instead of using *their* money, but they never mention it.

39

They know how I love my home. When I go, it will be theirs. Believe me, they've earned it."

Nannie had no money? Mom and Dad paid her bills?

Clues smashed into Brit's mind like trucks on the L.I.E. How could she not have tipped to it? This was the reason for the Honda with the 110,000 miles on it and the cut-rate tour to Alaska when their friends were driving a Lexus and taking upscale trips to European cities. "Mom really loves you," she whispered.

"Of course she does," said Nannie impatiently. "Even if she did rob me of all freedom and hope when she snatched my license and sold my car. Now. How are we going to find Flo?"

"Well, that would be the miracle of the twentieth century," said Brit. "Your century, I might add, not mine. It's an invention called the telephone."

Nannie giggled.

Directory assistance kindly located the phone number for Mrs. Arnold Heff.

"Flo's retirement center turned out to be a year-round slumber party," said Nannie, "where the girls play cards all the time and run book groups and tutor ESL students in the schools and have foreign affairs discussion clubs. All the men are dead, of course."

Brit was horrified. "How did they die?"

"How do men usually die? Strokes. Cardiac arrest. Men don't last long. Women always have another decade in them."

And then Brit was on the phone with Flo. "You're who?" bellowed Flo. "Doing what?"

"Brit Bowman!" she shouted back. "Nannie's granddaughter! I'm driving!"

"I'm not deaf!" Flo screamed back. "No need to shout!"

"She is too deaf," said Nannie. "Tell her not to forget her ears."

"I'm hard to find!" shouted Flo. "Stay on the phone and I'll give you turn-by-turn directions."

"I thought it was illegal in New York State to talk on your phone while you're driving!"

"Adds to the excitement!" yelled Flo.

Brit turned easily in the big pebbly space that now belonged to a land trust. How was she going to balance a phone and still go up and down those curly little hills? Brit was so ready to reach Flo's house. Even Coop receded from her mind. She needed a Coke, and nothing diet or caffeine free either. She needed lunch. Above all, she needed to powder her nose.

This is what it is to be eighty-six, Brit thought. You can't drive another mile, you're brain-dead and nothing matters except the potty.

"Brit!" shouted Flo. "Do you see a big yellow medical building with red doors straight in front of you?"

"Yes! Which way do I turn?"

"You don't. I'm just pointing it out. It's my doctor's office."

Brit had a spark of sympathy for George and Danielle.

"Okay!" Flo shouted. "Do you see an old gray shack that looks as if the pilgrims built it?"

"Yes," said Brit gloomily. Probably Flo's periodontist.

"That's my corner. Turn right. I'll stand out in front of my unit and wave."

Nannie took off her sunglasses. She primped her hair. She reapplied her lipstick. "We're almost there," she whispered.

★ ★ ★

Flo dyed her hair. It was faintly orange, and she wore makeup to match. Her shirt and trousers were very bright, her scarf jaunty and her sunglasses leopard-spotted. She was surrounded by old-fashioned scuffed leather baggage. "Her Buttermere luggage," said Nannie.

Imagine keeping the same luggage for sixty-five years. What was the point of having millions of dollars of waterfront property if you didn't go to the mall?

Flo was a tall bony woman. The outline of her jaw and nose had not softened with age like Nannie's but sharpened. She launched herself like a battleship upon the little rowboat that was Nannie. After they hugged and kissed, Flo turned to Brit. "How beautiful you are, darling. How lovely to be sixteen. And what a shame you're now a criminal, illegally driving rental cars."

Brit didn't want to address criminal issues. "Nannie and I need to powder our noses."

"She makes you talk like that?" said Flo. "Don't the other kids turn on you?"

Flo's apartment was rich with color. The paintings were very contemporary and the rugs were astonishing. Brit wanted to have an art lesson, but Flo was in a hurry. "Pick up the pace, girls. One potty trip and we hit the road."

"The road?" said Brit. "Aren't we going to spend the night? Or at least have lunch?"

"No time," said Flo, looking excited and orange. "It's summer and our reservations are for two-fifteen."

It seemed a rather late lunch for Nannie, who generally had dinner at five or even four-thirty, to get the Early Bird Senior Special.

"By nightfall," said Flo dramatically, "we will be in place to rescue our darling Aurelia Gibbs from that filthy worthless boy Aston."

Brit had forgotten the son's name. Aston. In fact, Aston 3, because his father had been Aston junior.

"It's good you're driving a heavy vehicle," Flo told Brit. "If Aston Three shows up, run over his feet and break all those little bones. He's not getting any younger, so his bones will never heal properly and they'll ache in wet weather for years to come." Flo nodded with satisfaction.

As soon as Flo and Nannie were seated at the restaurant, Brit would come back to the van, and in private, she could risk texting Coop. Something casual like *u rang?*

Then she'd answer everybody else's messages too, so she wouldn't feel that awful when Coop didn't respond.

Brit rearranged the beach chairs and set Flo's four suitcases in the van next to Nannie's. "And my pillows," directed Flo. "I travel with my own pillows or I don't get a minute's sleep."

Brit flung the pillows into a back seat and set the footstool by the sliding door of the Safari.

Nannie emerged from the bathroom and embarked upon a full report of what she had accomplished.

"Nannie!" shrieked Brit. "Stop it! Nobody wants to know!"

"I do," protested Flo.

"Not in front of me!"

They ignored her. Details were brought forward and experiences shared.

"Stop!" screamed Brit. "Grow up!"

"To be told at eighty-six that I must grow up. How lovely," Flo said to Nannie. "Your choice of chauffeur is excellent."

Brit plugged in their seat belts and slid behind the wheel.

Then she realized that to exit from Flo's condo, she had to back up. She climbed out, walked around the Safari and studied the situation. No cars, curbs, fire hydrants or pink blooming bushes were directly behind her. If she backed up absolutely straight for the length of the Safari plus another half length and then yanked the wheel to the right, she might get out of there without hitting anything.

She sat behind the wheel again.

"Can't back up?" Flo asked Nannie.

"No, but she's had her license only eleven days."

"Uh-oh," said Flo. "We're trusting her with our lives."

"Everything is a risk," agreed Nannie.

CHAPTER 4

"**I** wanted to kill my own daughter," said Brit's sweet pacifist grandmother. "Taking my license like that! Do you know what she said this morning? 'You're eighty-six,' she said. 'You don't have plans.'"

"Kill her," agreed Flo, and then screamed, "Turn left, Brit! No, no, too fast on that corner. Slow down going into a turn and accelerate coming out of it, Brittany Anne, and look out for the bicycle. Wait. Wait! Okay. Now go."

Brit was already totally sick of the girls and she had just two of them. What would it be like with four backseat drivers? Especially one with a walker? Especially when Flo

45

wasn't directing her to a restaurant at all but into a cemetery?

Row on row, spaced like squares on graph paper, stood identical grave markers, like inventory at a discount store. What a terrible place to spend eternity. "Stop here," said Flo.

Brit stopped. She lowered the windows a crack. Chilly damp air blew through the car. Graveyard weather.

Brit read the name and dates on the nearest marker. It had a flag. Lenny, who had died in Vietnam.

"Once I'm gone," said Flo, "nobody will know who Lenny was or how much he mattered." "Once I'm gone" meant "when I'm dead," words Nannie never used. You could admit you would be gone. You could not admit that you would not be coming back.

Brit looked in the rearview mirror, like a parent checking out the behavior of children in car seats. Nannie's hand slid into Flo's, and their age-spotted, blue-veined fingers twined together between the seats. Flo could visit her dead son only here, in this awful place, and that had been true for more than thirty years. And Brit was sulking because Flo was a backseat driver?

"Drive on, Brit," said Flo. "We're going to Port Jefferson."

This turned out to be a tourist town where T-shirts and tawdry earrings were sold on the sidewalks and crowds of pedestrians filled the streets. Every single one sensed that Brit did not know how to maneuver and they took total advantage. She came to a helpless halt while kids on bikes, shoppers with bags and fathers carrying babies in backpacks swarmed around her bumpers.

"Turn right!" shouted Flo. "Mow these people down if necessary!"

Brit turned right, hoping it would not be necessary. She hoped even more that their lunch reservation was still waiting, because she was starving to death. She found herself in a parking lot littered with young men. "Reservations?" asked a really cute one.

"Yes!" shrieked Flo from the backseat, and they checked Flo off on a clipboard and directed Brit to drive here, and then drive there, and then circle around the other way. What kind of restaurant treated patrons like this?

And then Brit saw that she was about to drive into the dark gaping maw of a car ferry. There was no restaurant and no time to use her cell phone. There was no car in front of her either, so she couldn't copy anybody else's method of getting onto this ferry. A crew member motioned her forward with such a glare that Brit figured he'd slice her tires if she didn't move along. The gangplank was a huge rattling metal street. Inside, the shadow was impenetrable. She sat until her eyes adjusted and the crew, outraged by this hesitation, began screaming at her. Cars were being divided into two groups: the people who drove straight ahead and tucked themselves neatly to the left or right . . . and the people who had to drive up a slanted metal hill and park on an upper level. The crew motioned Brit upward.

No! The slanted metal was way too steep; gravity would pull her off; she'd somersault; she'd crush some car below her, undoubtedly one with a sleeping newborn baby. The crew glared, and gestured.

"You know how we passed the time on the drive to your house?" Nannie said happily to Flo. "We sang 'She'll be comin' round the mountain when she comes.'" The girls burst into song. The crew looked incredulously at Brit, who put the windows up so nobody could hear more singing from two ancient grannies without voices. She assaulted the hill and got to park on the flat part at the top. She had just started to relax when she saw that some cars had to park on the downhill side, facing the exit, which was just an open wall of ship! Nothing between the front end of their cars and the deep cold black water except a chain that wouldn't stop a Doberman, let alone a van.

To leave this horrible ferry, she would have to drive down that vertical ramp, which meant using the brake very carefully, and as for the gas—how did a person use the gas when going downhill into the ocean?

A very handsome boy pounded on her window and yelled, "Set your parking brake!" Brit did not have the remotest idea where her parking brake was. She would have to sit here for the whole trip with her right foot holding the regular brake down. She hated being a jerk. Now she was a jerk in public in front of cute guys.

Nice summer vacation.

"It's on your left," said Flo. "Low down, under the dashboard."

Brit shoved the pedal so hard she practically put her foot through the floor. Then she unloaded her two grannies and guided them up open metal stairs toward the deck. Flo gripped the handrail with her good left hand while Brit held Nannie's arm and Nannie cried out usefully, "Don't fall! Don't fall!"

Of course as soon as they reached the top step, Nannie wanted to powder her nose.

Brit hated Flo and Nannie now and didn't care whether they ever found the bathroom.

Mom had been trying forever to get Nannie to stop saying "the girls" and start saying "the women." Nannie used the word "women" only when reading out loud the sign on a bathroom door, and even then she might reinterpret it and say "ladies." Nannie thought it was so funny when Mom asked, "Are you women getting together again?"

"We're the girls," Nannie would correct her gently.

Brit was sweaty and trembling, probably had tearstains, mascara running down her cheeks in black threads. Every kid who had crossed the Throgs Neck Bridge to get here was saying, "Mommy, what is a throg?" and Mommy was pointing at Brit.

Brit directed the girls toward the sign that said WOMEN. Then she staggered out to the open deck, where dozens of molded green plastic chairs were scattered, and fell into one. She didn't save chairs for Flo and Nannie. Let them stand. The reason nobody else was sitting became clear. Puddles had collected in the seats of the chairs.

Brit was not just a throg's neck; she was a throg's neck who had wet her pants.

Flo tottered up. "Nannie and I will be sitting inside," said Flo. "Right behind you. Just so you don't worry."

"I wasn't worrying," said Brit. These women should be on their knees with gratitude instead of siccing ferries on her. Maybe she would just give the car keys to some cute crew member, saying, "Not only do you get a nice new van with cup holders, it comes equipped with backseat drivers."

"How refreshing," said Flo. "I think it's the least attractive thing about being eighty-six, and believe me, it's filled with unattractive things. People are always worrying about you, and you're always having to shout, 'I'm fine! Go away!'"

Indeed, Brit yearned to shout, "I'm fine! Go away!"

And finally Flo did.

The ferry headed out to sea and turned itself around, and now Brit was facing backward. Everybody went to the other end of the boat to watch Connecticut appear on the far horizon.

Brit gazed at the waves. She considered the sky. She studied Coop's digital remains.

She had not often been in a class with him, but senior year they'd be in calculus together because there was only one section. She felt too dumb for calculus. She was a person who couldn't even find a parking brake.

Quick as diving into ice water, she called Coop. With her voice. Out loud.

His mother answered.

What was his mother doing answering his cell phone? That was what cell phones were all about: your mother didn't answer them. "Hi, Mrs. James," she said helplessly. "How are you?"

"Who's this?"

"Brit Bowman. I'm returning Coop's call. Is he at home?"

"Oh," said his mother. "Hello, Brittany Anne."

What was with these people who could not call her by the name she herself had just used? How could people she barely knew, like Mrs. James, remember her middle name? Shouldn't they be too busy to remember things like that?

"Cooper's doing chores," said Mrs. James in a hostile voice. "I'll tell him you called." Mrs. James hung up.

Brit wanted to break the phone in half or maybe smash a large piece of furniture. All furniture on the boat was either plastic or bolted to the deck. She tried to think of a good way to calm down other than hurling herself overboard.

The phone rang in her hand. Her old cell phone had had a little icon of an old-fashioned black desk phone that shimmied whenever there was an incoming call. Brit had always shimmied along. Her current phone had a camera but no shimmy. If this was Coop, Brit would shimmy anyway.

But it was not Cooper James. It was Hayley. "Hi, Britsy."

"I've told you for ten years not to call me Britsy."

"You lose. Now what's happening? Did you find a driver?"

"That would be me," said Brit. "I'm driving Nannie to her college reunion. We've already picked up roommate number one and we're leaving Long Island on the car ferry and Cooper James is trying to reach me on the phone."

"Coop?" screamed Hayley. "That's fabulous! Hang up on me right now! Get hold of him! Then call me back instantly and tell me what he wanted. He has to want to do something with you. It has to be a movie. There's nothing else to do in this weather."

"He didn't leave a message," said Brit.

"That's because he's a boy. Boys don't understand the necessity of messages. He figures he'll get back to you and he's forgotten about caller ID and he didn't stop to think that you know he called and you're thinking of nothing else and now he's probably digging up a garden for his mother because that's the kind of thing Mrs. James makes him do when normal people are hanging out at the mall. I've been on that ferry. It takes an hour. Plenty of time to reach Cooper and call me back." Hayley disconnected.

Brit hadn't exactly lied to Hayley, but she'd skipped stuff, like the fact that she'd already tried and gotten Mrs. James instead. That kind of thing would never happen to Hayley. Brit wanted to turn the phone off so she wouldn't have to deal with a call-back from Hayley, but then she couldn't get a callback from Coop either.

The phone rang again. Dum dum dum daaaaahhhh. Brit had forgotten her parents even existed, let alone were en route to Alaska. "Hi, darling. You wouldn't believe it. We're only just now airborne. The seats are terrible. Your father's knees don't fit. And it's so cloudy that even though I have a window seat I can't see America."

When that was finally over and Brit was off the phone and the line was free for Cooper to call, of course nothing happened. The wind picked up. She was going to get hypothermia and freeze to death in Connecticut in June.

And then Cooper called back.

She made absolutely sure there was no camera availability through which Coop could see what a throg's neck she was right now.

Another ring went by. If she missed Coop a second time, she would throw herself overboard and let the gulls peck on her. She took a deep breath. "Hi, Coop." What if he asked her out on a weekend when she had a van full of old ladies making potty stops?

"Hey, Brit. I'm sorry I bothered you. I heard on the scanner that some sort of crime happened at your grandmother's house and the police were there, so I called your house and there was no answer, so I called your number, but right then, my mother got a call from Lindsay Dorrelle explaining that you destroyed your own grandmother's lawn."

"I did not! Nannie did!"

"The police told Lindsay Dorrelle that you confessed."

"I had to cover for Nannie. She got a rental car, see, and she couldn't drive it because she's too short, and she totally tore up her own yard because she got the brake and the gas mixed up. But I couldn't tell the police what really happened because we needed the rental car to get to Nannie's college reunion."

"Her best driving is going in circles through her own flower beds and you're letting her out on the highway?"

"No, no, I'm driving."

"How can *you* drive a rental car?"

"Well—illegally."

They both laughed.

"All drivers!" screamed the speakers, as loud as chainsaws. "Back to your cars!"

"What's that?" said Coop.

"I'm on the Port Jeff Ferry."

"Oh. It sounded like the end of recreation at a maximum-security prison."

"I've scheduled prison for tomorrow. Today I'm just an illegal driver of a rental car, but in the morning, I'm going to kidnap a friend of my grandmother's."

"Not too shabby," said Coop. "All I have scheduled is another bowl of cold cereal."

"All drivers!" shrieked the loudspeaker. A torrent of people spilled from other decks and flooded the stairwells as they rushed to their cars. From behind glass doors, Flo and Nannie waved wildly, as if Brit would otherwise forget them. "I have to go," said Brit.

"Wait! I need details on the kidnapping."

And suddenly, instead of enjoying the laugh they'd just shared, Brit became furious with stupid old Cooper James. What was up with him—holding a grudge for six months just because he'd found out that she liked him? How dare he trespass inside her personal laptop anyway? How dare he not even say thank you after she signed his stupid yearbook? How dare he chat away right now like an old friend when in fact he was a creep who publicly gagged at the thought of her? "See you in calculus," she said, which meant next year.

She'd better be back in that van in a hurry if she planned to study how everybody else was getting down that ramp and off the ferry. She galloped toward Flo and Nannie.

Nannie, however, refused to be on the stairs while all those people were hurrying down; she might get knocked over. Flo agreed. There might be a rogue wave and she would be flung to the floor far below, where she would break her *left* side, in which case she would be helpless and have to spend the rest of her life lying in some sterile environment, being fed by a tube.

Brit shouted for a crew member to help Flo and Nannie down.

Flo's hearing aids began to whistle. The high thin screech pierced Brit's ears like knitting needles.

"I hate these," said Flo, who certainly couldn't hate them as much as every other passenger on the ferry.

"Throw them overboard," advised Nannie.

"Good idea," said Flo, and she did. The hearing aids arced out over Long Island Sound. Seagulls rushed forward, in case these were old French fries to scarf up, but the hearing aids hit the water and presumably sank forever. "I was once quite a softball pitcher," Flo informed Brit.

A young man from the crew rushed up. "Gotta hurry. You don't get your car started, you're gonna block a hundred cars that wanna get off, you understand? People aren't patient in the summer, you understand?"

Brit understood.

Her phone rang.

It was Cooper wanting to know why she had hung up on him and what calculus had to do with anything, except that she was obviously making lousy calculations about her driving future. "I can't talk!" she yelled. "I have to figure out how to drive off the ferry without driving into the water and drowning us!"

"Open your windows," advised Coop. "That way, if you do drive into the water and the electrical system in your car is compromised, you won't be sealed in. You can swim ashore."

Nannie turned on the stairs to see why Brit was laughing. The ferry hit the pilings of the dock, the boat jerked hard and Nannie fell.

Brit dropped her phone and leaped down three steps to grab her grandmother. She got a piece of mauve jacket but Nannie slid out of it. Flo screamed. The crew guy, like Brit, was left holding a sleeve. Brit screamed too.

Another passenger whirled on the steps and caught Nannie in his arms, but her slight weight unbalanced him, and they fell backward. The guy caught himself on the railings and cushioned Nannie's fall.

"Are you all right?" Flo screamed.

"Are you all right?" the crew guy screamed, pulling them to their feet and dusting them off.

"We're fine," said the catcher, proud of his save.

"We're fine," said Nannie. But she wasn't fine. She was trembling and pale, almost green, as one about to faint. Her fingers locked on Brit's arm, and her tears spilled over.

What am I doing? thought Brit. Nannie could have gotten hurt while I was in charge. In fact, she could get hurt *because* I'm in charge. I'm letting her do really stupid things. She's old. She's breakable. I could have killed us a hundred times on the L.I.E. because I just don't have the experience for that kind of road—and now I'm supposed to do even more driving? And we can't go and kidnap somebody! Aurelia's son knows what's right for his mother.

Mom's right, thought Brit. Nannie is losing her marbles if she thinks for one minute we can actually do this.

"Thank you," she said to the passenger who had caught Nannie.

This nutty plan could only get nuttier. Nannie had already done more today than she usually did in a month. What if Brit went ahead with this insane stuff and looked in her rearview mirror and Nannie was having a heart attack?

More crew came running up to make sure Nannie was okay, which would have been more helpful five minutes before. Brit could have used a crew member's arm herself. But nobody offered one. Either she looked pretty sturdy or else a throg's neck didn't get help.

She looked at her watch. They hadn't even had lunch yet, and it was three-thirty.

Her head began to throb. The ferry was landing in Bridgeport, Connecticut, a city so grim that nobody ever went there, they only left it. But it was just ten or twenty easy miles from home via I-95.

Heavily escorted, they reached the Safari. The crew boosted Flo and Nannie into the back. Brit fixed the girls' seat belts and slid forward into the driver's seat. Every engine around them was roaring and every window was down and every radio station on earth was playing at full volume and everything echoed in the metal chamber of the ferry . . . and Brit could not release the parking brake.

She pushed. She pulled. She kicked.

Nothing happened.

"Britsy?" called Nannie.

"Later!" She yanked harder. A hundred cars were going to be stuck behind her. The crew was going to trot over and yell through the window, "Take off that parking brake, dummy," while she sat there whimpering.

"Brit?" called Flo.

"In a minute!" screamed Brit.

But without her hearing aids, Flo didn't hear and just kept on talking. "Once we're off the ferry, don't get on the interstate. Follow the signs for the Route Eight Connector."

Brit yanked. Still no result.

The crew will have to help me, she thought. They'll want to see the rental car paperwork and my license and they'll call the police and Nannie will be so dithery, I'll be put in juvenile detention until the police reach Mom and Dad in Alaska. And when that's over, it won't be over; Mom and Dad will never let me drive again. I'll never be able to afford car insurance on my own. If I can't drive, I'm nobody. I can't go anywhere or do anything. I'll have to wait for college to be a person.

"Aurelia is about two hours north, Brit," said Flo happily. "It's an easy straight drive up Route Eight."

"We're not going there. We're going back to Nannie's." Brit would get the car safely into Nannie's driveway and call the rental car people to pick it up and this would be over and there would be no evidence. Except the lawn, of course. And the fact that Lindsay Dorrelle had telephoned the entire world with the news that Brit was her own grandmother's vandal and Mrs. James was now so revolted by Brit she couldn't even stay on a phone with her.

"What are you talking about?" said Nannie. "We can't go home. We have to get Aurelia."

"I don't care about Aurelia. Mom told me to take care of you. I haven't been doing that. You could have gotten hurt."

"I do not need to be taken care of. And I was not hurt. Aurelia needs us."

"No. We're driving where I say we're driving. And that's home."

Cars on the lower level began to move off the ferry. Crew motioned each row forward and each car leaped to obey.

"Aurelia is expecting us!" cried Flo. "We are her last and only hope!"

The crew motioned Brit's line forward. She gave the parking brake one last violent heave and it disengaged. The Safari inched forward with the gas it gave itself and crept down the vertical parking slot. Brit was crying now and had to wipe the stupid tears away with the back of her hand so she could see where the ramp went. She was going too fast. Now that she had spent all this energy getting rid of one brake, she had to use the other brake to slow down. She tapped it with her right toe and accomplished nothing. She jammed it down and the van lurched and skidded. The crew looked at her with disgust. She let up on the brake a speck but the van remained motionless. She let up a little more and went downhill so fast she all but slammed the bumper ahead of her and this time she braked so hard the girls probably got whiplash.

When she bottomed out, Brit was so afraid to steer between the various barriers, it took three guys to gesture her onto the off-ramp. If she ever had to go to Long Island again, she was taking the train.

"We have to get Aurelia!" Nannie cried.

"Shut up," whispered Brit.

Knuckles rapped sharply on her window. She didn't drive off the ferry into the water only because her foot was on the brake, not the accelerator. The guy who'd let Nannie fall was grinning through the window.

Brit could barely remember how to get a window down. She definitely couldn't remember how to grin.

"Your cell phone," he said when she finally located the window controls. "It fell under the stairs. I've been looking for it all this time."

She had to wet her lips twice to manage a thank-you.

"Drive carefully now," he said, snickering. She looked around to see the entire crew snickering at her pathetic driving. Brit tossed the phone on the empty passenger seat and drove off the ferry.

"Brit, we need you," said her grandmother. "This matters so much. Please. Without you, it can't be done."

Brit was at a four-way stop. A sign pointed to I-95, which would take them home. I'm the driver, she thought. They can whine all they want, like toddlers in car seats, but the driver wins. "No, Nannie."

One by one, cars took their turns through the intersection.

Brit checked her rearview mirror. Nannie was as white and crumpled as a discarded paper napkin. Flo looked like an orange-stained rag. Their heads lolled as if the weight of their thoughts was too much to hold up.

I did that, thought Brit. I'm young, I'm powerful. They're old, they're weak. Shove over—that's my new theme song. You're old, I'm young, you lose.

"If you won't think of me," said her grandmother, "please think of Aurelia."

Brit didn't want to think of this old crone she had never met. She wanted a hot shower and a change of clothing and lunch, for heaven's sake, and no risk, none at all, none whatsoever, to her personal driving future.

But she thought of Aurelia anyhow. Going to church that Sunday. Happy to have her son home, happy that she could take his strong arm instead of her walker. Perhaps she'd enjoyed the sermon and shaken the minister's hand after the service and paraded slowly to Aston's car, looking forward to brunch at some delightful restaurant. Looking forward to her son's good company and conversation.

And then—puzzlement. "Aston, dear?"

And he—courteous; the people in charge can always afford to be courteous. "Yes, Mother?"

"Where are we going?"

And her son, her only son on this earth: "A nursing home, Mother. I'm selling your house. You're being institutionalized. You aren't competent. I'll be handling your money."

Aurelia had not been able to say good-bye to her friends and neighbors. She had not been able to resign from her committees or her bridge group. Not been able to use up the milk in the refrigerator, pack her own clothes or choose for herself the only possessions she could keep for the rest of her life in a single room.

But above all, Aurelia Gibbs had not been able to make Aston 3 turn around. The driver chose the destination. The weak and frail in the back had no say.

What if Coop called one more time? *And then what did you do?* he would ask Brit. And she would say to him, *I threw in the towel. So what? They're old.*

She thought of the sixteen years Nannie had spent bringing her up.

Ahead of her, the light was green.

Brit followed the signs for Route 8 and went north to kidnap Aurelia.

CHAPTER 5

The terrible moment in which a sixteen-year-old put two grandmothers in their place was over. But Brit had proved that she was the grown-up. Flo and Nannie were the children who could only hope for good treatment. But Brit didn't yell to the backseat that she was sorry. There was nothing Brit hated more than saying she was sorry. She would rather sulk for weeks than admit to being wrong. Anyway, she wasn't sorry. Going home would be the right choice. She was letting Nannie make the wrong choice and they both knew it.

She was shocked by her own thought—*letting* Nannie make a choice.

So when you got old . . . it wasn't like being sixteen, when people said, "If she makes the wrong choice, she'll learn from it." When you got old, you didn't get to choose. If there was a choice, somebody might let you make it or they might not.

She didn't want to think about grandmothers anymore. She drove on and on, past ugly mill towns and streams surging over their banks with spring rain. Eventually she reached for the phone on the front passenger seat. There was a law against *talking* on the phone while driving, but maybe it was okay to *listen*.

FIRST NEW VOICE MESSAGE:

"Brit! What's going on? Did you really and truly drive off the ferry into the water? That's what it sounded like! Are you okay? I assume the ferry crew is trained in submerged-car rescue, though. Call me back!"

SECOND NEW VOICE MESSAGE:

"Brit, darling, we're over one of the Great Lakes. The sky has cleared! No rain, no clouds. Did you and Nannie find your jelly doughnuts?"

THIRD NEW VOICE MESSAGE:

"No fair turning off your cell phone. I need to know if you're alive. Unless your phone is lying in the mud at the bottom of Long Island Sound and so are you, in which case I'm actually talking to a dead woman. Come on, Brit, call me back."

FOURTH NEW VOICE MESSAGE:

"Well? What did Cooper say? What did he want? No fair not telling. I'm dying of boredom. And you know that I start my summer job this afternoon, and even though it's raining out and nobody buys ice cream in the rain, and this kind of temperature doesn't even qualify as summer, I have to work at the Dairy

Queen and serve ice cream. But if Cooper is speaking to you again, I need to know. It'll give me something wonderful and romantic to think about while I'm dipping cones in chocolate."

FIRST NEW TEXT MESSAGE:

Hi. day 1 vac. bored. Amanda.

Brit was many things right now but not bored. She would have figured that if she drowned ten times over, Coop wouldn't care. He had actually left two voice messages to check on her dead-or-alive status?

They had been on Route 8 an hour, and now the woods were deep, and the hills rising. Nannie said in a trembly voice, "Brit? Perhaps we could find a place where I could powder my nose?"

Shame flooded Brit. She knew her grandmother's constant need, but had she bothered? No. She had forced Nannie to ask.

There was no place to powder a nose here except behind a bush. She drove on and on, feeling guiltier and guiltier, until at last the divided highway ended and Route 8 became a regular country road. Right where they should be—the people at McDonald's knew their stuff—were golden arches. "McDonald's always has clean bathrooms," said Brit. "And I really think we all have to have some lunch or we'll be sick." Not that you could call it lunch at four-thirty.

"My treat," said Flo quickly. "I'm in a hamburger mood."

"Me too!" cried Nannie, who was never in a hamburger mood.

They have no gifts to bring, thought Brit. They'll grovel for the rest of this trip, because otherwise this trip can't happen. I'm not on their team now; they'll never think of me as being on their team. I'm the grown-up and they have to be nice to me and beg. "We can look for a real restaurant," she offered.

"No, no!" cried Nannie. "McDonald's is perfect, Brit!"

★ ★ ★

After hamburgers, fries and shakes, Nannie and Flo slept in their bucket seats, cushioned in the feathery depths of Flo's special pillows, while Brit drove north into Massachusetts. Flo had jotted down the directions on the back of an old envelope.

The envelope killed Brit.

Flo and Nannie had lived through the 1930s, a decade called the Depression. For them, "depression" did not mean a mental condition requiring counseling. It meant poverty and fear. Losing a job, losing a home, going without, your children going without—perhaps just without shoes but maybe also without lunch or dinner. And even though their own families had not suffered badly, the Depression was still with them. Here was Flo—born in wealth, stayed in wealth, made wealth of her own—not buying cute little notepads on which to write directions, but instead saving her old envelopes.

Brit checked her mirror. Flo and Nannie were breathing slowly, eyes and cheeks sunk in the way of toddlers deep into naps. She was as alone as she was going to get. She called Coop.

One thing about caller ID—you could start the conversation in the middle because the other person knew who you were. "It's about time," said Coop, starting the conversation in the middle.

"See, first my grandmother fell down the ferry stairs and while I was trying to catch her I dropped my cell phone, which probably hit every single metal step going down, and that was what you heard. Then, by the time the crew found it, you were listening to a couple hundred engines and car radios. I couldn't get the parking brake off, so I was too busy to answer phones and when I drove off the ferry—"

"You didn't drive into the water, then?" said Coop.

"Don't sound so disappointed."

"I wanted to film you hurtling off the side and your car sinking and your fingernails scratching at the window as you ran out of air and at the last second you'd be hauled out, and we'd air it nationwide and you'd be famous as the dripping-wet, almost dead girl, and I'd be famous as the brilliant cameraman."

"I don't plan to be famous as an almost dead person," said Brit. "And you could at least dream of saving me yourself, instead of filming somebody else's save. Anyway, I turned out to be a much better driver than that." This was untrue, as she had barely gotten on and off the ferry alive, but on the phone with a boy, especially a boy who was never going to be allowed to drive and could only envy those who *were* drivers, it was okay to embellish.

"I'm not even driving in my driveway," said Cooper gloomily. "When's the kidnap?"

"Tomorrow morning."

"Where?"

"Why? Are you going to alert the authorities so they can cut me off?"

"No. I just need something to think about since I have nothing to do. I'm working for a landscape architect, but it's too wet to move dirt. I'm building a screened porch with my dad, but it's too wet to pour footings. I have a new bike and Ben and I mapped out day trips, but there it is again. Rain. Meanwhile, you're . . ." He struggled for a phrase.

"Following in Rupert's footsteps," said Brit.

"I hope not. Rupert generally gets caught. You'll want to skip that part. Now catch me up on this illegal driving."

"My mother sold Nannie's Cadillac because she's eighty-six

65

and she can't see or brake, but Nannie needed transportation, so she just rented a car. But then the Safari they delivered was too big for her to drive. So I'm driving."

"If I was lucky enough to have a driver's license," said Coop, "I wouldn't do anything to jeopardize it. Rupert was always happy to jeopardize anything, but I wouldn't have cast you as a Rupert."

In the midst of wet maples and sorrowful cows huddled in fields was a large sign for I-90. Brit checked Flo's envelope, which said to go west on the Mass Pike. It was possible that I-90 and the Mass Pike were the same thing, like the L.I.E. and the Long Island Expressway. It was also possible that in rural quiet western Massachusetts there were two interstates serving some vast invisible population. "I think I have to make a crucial turn," said Brit.

"Okay." Coop disconnected, his interest used up now that she hadn't drowned.

There was an entrance ramp, so she took it. Yesterday, Brit wouldn't have gotten on an interstate at all, never mind risked getting on the wrong one. She drove west on I-90, and eventually, a sign confirmed that it was also the Mass Pike. No traffic. It was all this rain. People weren't having ice cream and they weren't crossing state lines.

Dum dum dum daaaahhhh.

Brit had lost all sense of time. Maybe her parents had reached Alaska. She felt as if she had driven to Alaska today: mined it, settled it, gotten it statehood.

No, they hadn't gotten to Alaska, Mom reported. They had just reached Seattle, where they would change planes, but it was a long layover. When at last Mom stopped talking, she put Dad on the phone, and Dad was not a great talker, so it was Brit's responsibility to talk when Dad was on the phone. She had to do this without letting them suspect the existence of a car, a road trip or a destination.

She reached the Route 7 exit (New England seemed to have a pretty basic numbering system), said good-bye to Dad, who was just as glad to hang up as she was, and followed the envelope instructions south to yet another quaint white-clapboard village: Stockbridge.

Brit was not drawn to quaint. She wanted Manhattan. She wanted to wear black. She wanted to stalk down sidewalks in fashionable high heels. She wanted to run out of space in her walk-in closets because they were jammed with so many great clothes. She wanted to go to clubs and fine restaurants after work, and her work would be glamorous and she would become a celebrity and people like Cooper would follow her around, earning lots of money selling clips of her.

The Red Lion Inn, where Flo had made their reservations, was big and white. On its deep front porch were pots of begonias (old-lady flowers) and white wicker rockers (old-lady chairs) with lots of old ladies in them. Rocking.

All of a sudden Brit was so exhausted by the driving and by the girls, she could hardly stand looking at them. She wanted to scream and kick something. Instead she had to wake them gently, help their stiff bodies stir from a sitting position, and shift them onto the stepstool. They were much more frightened of falling than they had been before the ferry stair incident.

Flo had made reservations for only one room—the double Flo and Nannie would share. She had not anticipated the presence of Brit. "I'm sorry," chirped the desk clerk. "We're full. No more rooms."

Nannie and Flo looked at Brit with genuine fear. The

essential driver—who could turn on them at any moment—had nowhere to stay.

"It doesn't matter," said Brit, putting on fake cheer like stage makeup. "Can you put a cot in the room for me?" she asked, although a better fate would have been falling off the ferry and drowning. If they shared a room, she couldn't call Hayley, and conversations with boys were nothing until they were shared with a girlfriend. And if she was in the same room as Nannie and Flo, they'd want the television off by eight-thirty and probably wouldn't watch anything but nature shows on PBS anyway.

"A cot," agreed the clerk. "And if we have a cancellation, we'll give you a room of your own."

Brit registered a prayer with God that a cancellation would be a really good thing.

Very clearly, she heard God say, Since when do you deserve a really good thing? You're displaying mental cruelty toward your own grandmother and you want a reward?

These little one-sided conversations happened from time to time. Brit knew it was her conscience, but she also knew it was God nosing in and watching. It was one of the things about God that was so unwelcome: He was always looking.

A porter got the suitcases. Brit parked the van out back, hoisted her backpack and even remembered Flo's pillows.

She had brought exactly one change of clothes and a toothbrush. Toothpaste was in the bathroom at Nannie's, and extra clothes were in the closet of the room where Brit normally slept at Nannie's; anything else she needed was at her own house, a five-minute drive when the aide came, or a twenty-minute walk if she felt like it. She had no makeup with her. She had no shoes except the dirty sneakers. No earrings. She was a real product person, and here she was without her own skin cleanser or her own shampoo or her own conditioner.

All Brit possessed right now was a really bad mood.

★ ★ ★

Even though they had had a cancellation and Brit got her own room, she couldn't sleep. At dawn she went for her run.

Sometimes she loved running. She loved the shape of her body and the length of her stride, the taste of the weather and the image of herself as an athlete. This was not one of those times.

Gloomy clouds whipped over a pale sky, and passing cars tossed puddle water on her legs. Back at the hotel, Brit took a shower, dried her hair with the hotel blow dryer and put on the same yucky jeans and sweatshirt. She left a message on Mom's voice mail, then called her own house and also Nannie's to delete any messages left by Lindsay Dorrelle, which Mom might check and have a heart attack about, and considered the day to come.

They weren't kidnapping anybody.

That was just Nannie's silly excited word. Brit didn't need duct tape or a ransom note. They were taking an old biddy out to lunch, not committing crimes. The girls would share a dessert, sip weak tea with skim milk and trundle on to a reunion, during which Brit would take out and put back that stepstool a million times.

Then she had a terrible thought.

It's not enough that I have to *take* them to the reunion. I'll have to *stay*. I'll have to listen to speeches about how American values and educational standards have declined and then they'll serve a casserole with canned peas in it.

She found the girls sitting on their beds, waiting for her.

Yesterday's outfits were deemed perhaps too casual for a nursing home snatch. Flo looked very New York in an elegant black skirt, an ivory silk blouse and a smashing red and black scarf. Nannie looked very country in a navy blue dress with fat white polka dots and a little round white collar.

"Good morning, darling," said Nannie brightly. "Flody and I talked way into the night." (Brit figured this meant nine-fifteen.) "And we were awake rather early." (This was certainly true and meant five a.m.) "And we took our medications and had room service breakfasts and we're ready to get Aurelia."

It was bravado. Nannie's smile was anxious and she was shivering. Flo, staring out the window at those ominous clouds scudding in that high wind, was folding and refolding a map. "Here we go," whispered Flo nervously.

"Did you have breakfast?" Nannie wanted to know.

The most Brit ever did for breakfast was brush her teeth. "I'm all set."

"Is that all you have to wear?" said her grandmother sadly.

"Yes," she snapped. It was not a good sign that she was totally out of patience and they hadn't left the hotel yet. "So where is Aurelia's nursing home?"

Flo held out another envelope on which driving instructions had been written. North on Route 7—same road Brit came in on. Continue north past the Mass Pike. A half dozen miles and a bunch of turns later, and she'd be at Fox Hills Adult Community.

In Nannie's kitchen hung a black-and-white photograph of the girls standing on the steps of Buttermere Dormitory for Young Ladies. They had their arms around each other and three of them were laughing. Those three looked oddly similar, with their pin-curled waves, flared skirts and pearl necklaces. Aurelia

70

was the small, dark, elegant one, staring soberly at the camera, as if she saw farther into the future than the others. Was Aurelia too sitting on the edge of her bed? Waiting? Scared?

Brit brought the car around and parked at the front steps of the Red Lion Inn.

It was colder than when she had taken her run. She put the heat on for the girls and distributed the car blankets Nannie had wisely included while a porter loaded both luggage and girls.

Brit clicked on 1010 WINS, impressed that she could get New York City reception up here, and discovered that this June was setting a record for the coldest, wettest June ever. Wonderful.

As soon as she got on 7 north, she came to a Citgo station and realized that she had never, not once, glanced at her gas gauge. She looked now. The needle was below E.

She imagined Nannie and Flo abandoned in this chilly van while she hiked back to a gas station or waited forever and a half for AAA. There was so much more to driving than she would have thought yesterday.

Of course by then she had driven past the gas station—had to find a side road, turn around, drive back—and then she didn't know which side of the car the gas tank was on and she guessed wrong and had to reposition.

At last she was on 7 again, headed north.

The rain paused. Cows sheltered under trees. Horses grazed behind fences. White houses wore black shutters. A scarlet cardinal swept around the curve ahead.

How serene it was. Only gentle and good things could happen here.

Unless you got caught kidnapping.

CHAPTER 6

Fox Hills Adult Community had no hills and no foxes, but it sure had parking. Maybe the builders expected every sick old person to have two cars and tons of visitors. Since none of them did, empty parking lots wrapped around long brick buildings. Brit parked in a visitor slot near the front door. "Does Aurelia know the plan?" she asked. She didn't like looking at the actual building. It meant they were actually going to do this.

"It's her plan," explained Nannie. "I called her last night and she knows you're driving. I will be Aurelia's sister. Flo will be our cousin. You will be my granddaughter."

Brit felt she could handle her part pretty well.

"We explain to the staff that we will be lunching at the Red Lion Inn," said Nannie breathlessly. "I even made reservations because I don't want to tell too many lies."

Brit helped the girls out of the car and carefully locked the Safari. Then she thought, What am I locking up for? We're the kidnappers. We don't have to worry about somebody else doing bad deeds.

Big glass doors opened automatically into a large foyer arranged like Brit's high school—principal's office to the left and a secretary blocking the way. Sure enough, the secretary looking up, frowning, satisfying the job description for school secretaries.

"Hi, there!" called Nannie. "We're here to take Aurelia Gibbs out to lunch."

"How nice for Mrs. Gibbs. Won't she have a lovely time. I'll telephone Dr. Gibbs for permission."

They needed a doctor's permission to take somebody out to lunch? And the doctor was the patient's own son? Nobody had said Aston 3 was a doctor! A doctor must know when his mother needed nursing home care. What if Aurelia was on oxygen or getting IV medication?

"I'm Aurelia's sister," Flo informed the secretary, forgetting that she was the cousin, "and we don't need to bother dear Aston. That's for strangers, of course."

"Oh?" The secretary made a big deal out of being puzzled, just like a school secretary who knows you're fibbing and wants you to sweat. "Dr. Gibbs never mentioned a sister," she said prissily. But then, maybe the woman had a right to wonder what kind of sister showed up for her first visit after Aurelia had been here six months.

Brit was an old hand at deceiving school secretaries. They liked inside information. "I'm the granddaughter," she said, giving the impression that she was also the only one who still had her marbles. "And of course I'm doing the driving." She and the secretary rolled their eyes at each other.

Right away the secretary was Brit's best friend. "Elevator to the second floor, down the hall to Building C. Mrs. Gibbs is in two-seventeen," she told Brit, ignoring Nannie and Flo. "I'll call Rose, her aide, so that Rose will be on the lookout for you."

"Thank you," said Brit, while Nannie cried, "Look! I see elevators!" Since Nannie now sounded like a nursery school tot hoping to be allowed to push the buttons, Brit and the secretary bonded by rolling their eyes a second time.

With eerie slowness, the elevator moved to the second floor. When the doors opened, Nannie stepped over the tiny crack of the elevator shaft the way she might cross a crevasse in a glacier. Gripping railings that ran the length of the corridor, Nannie and Flo set out. In single file, the three of them moved as if hauling themselves uphill on a rope.

Brit's cell phone rang.

Since Nannie had forgotten her hearing aids and Flo's were underwater, neither of the girls heard. Brit yanked her cell out of her pocket to shut it down, but it was Cooper James again. What was this all about? He couldn't talk to her for months on end and now he wanted to talk every five minutes? "Coop, I can't talk now."

"Are you pulling off the kidnapping this minute?"

"Yes."

"Tell me everything that happens."

"Kidnappers are busy people, Cooper. They can't be hanging out on the phone."

"Come on, Brit. It's raining again. I've already been on the

Internet, watched TV reruns, had a second breakfast and walked the dog. I'm bored."

"I'm lower on your list than walking the dog?"

"The dog gets up earlier," said Coop. "Just leave your phone on. We don't actually have to talk. I'll listen in. Is it a camera phone? I wouldn't mind receiving a few action pictures."

They were passing the numbered doors of patients' rooms. Some residents had hung paintings or WELCOME signs by their doors, but Brit didn't see anybody or hear anybody. "There's no such thing as an action picture here," she told Coop. "This place is like a dead zone for breathing people."

"Oh, Flody, did you hear what Britsy said?" cried Nannie. "A dead zone. I can hardly bear the thought of Aurelia living here. In a *dead* zone."

"We cannot waste time on pointless emotion," said Flo. "That desk clerk is going to call Aston."

Nannie nodded. "By the time we reach Rose, the jig could be up."

"The jig could be up?" repeated Coop, laughing.

Brit's heart hurt. Now she understood why Cooper was phoning. Not because he liked her. Because they were entertainment. Yesterday, she thought, the police were at Nannie's house, always fun. Then I was a possible drowning subject, and now Nannie and Flo and I—second to the dog, of course—are presenting a little sideshow. If only he could have action pictures to go with it.

Nannie looked back to make sure Brit was still there, her eyes glassy with tears and her wrinkles deepened by fear.

"Gotta go, Coop," said Brit. "Later." She turned the phone off and shoved it into her jeans pocket. How did people who bought pants without pockets survive?

Although Brit had pictured the aide as a stern hefty prison matron, Rose was a pretty young woman bouncing on tiptoe. "Mrs. Gibbs has been dressed for hours," Rose informed them, beaming. "I'm so glad something lovely is going to happen today and she isn't just confused the way she usually is."

Brit didn't like the sound of that. Flo and Nannie didn't like the sound of that. They looked at each other fearfully.

"I'll pop her into a wheelchair," said Rose, "and take her down to the front door for you, and one of you can bring her walker along. She'll need it to get in and out of the restaurant." Rose went into Room 217. "Mrs. Gibbs!" she yelled. "Visitors! Lunch!"

You had to talk to Aurelia in one-word sentences?

Brit was all done with this. But Nannie and Flo entered 217 and Brit could hardly wait out in the hall. She stood in the doorway.

The woman sitting on the edge of her hospital bed was elegantly dressed in a green wool suit. Her shoes matched. Her watchband was a narrow strip of apple green enamel and her delicate handbag was striped in three shimmering green shades. But her osteoporosis was so advanced she could hardly lift her head: her spine was curled like a candy cane. Her hair was thin and gray, her cheeks wrinkled and sagging. Swollen ankles lapped over the edges of her shoes. Her gnarled hands had a tremor that moved up her arms and neck and made her head bob.

Brit didn't even want to go into the room. She was not actually afraid of Aurelia—and yet she was, as if being very old and decrepit were catching.

"You came," whispered Aurelia, as if she had never really believed they would. She held out her hands to Nannie and Flo. *"You both came,"* she said, almost weeping. They air-hugged. Perhaps real hugs would snap Aurelia's brittle bones.

76

"Of course we came," said Nannie stoutly, and Brit hoped Nannie would never tell Aurelia they had almost failed her—because Brit had almost failed them. Even Nannie seemed appalled by how awful Aurelia looked. If this had ever been just an adventure, that was over. This was a nightmare. They were actually conniving to take a very sick old woman away from the medical care her doctor son had arranged.

With the gritty expression of one determined not to cry, Nannie propelled Brit closer. "And this, Aurelia, is my darling granddaughter, Brittany Anne."

Even harder than releasing that parking brake was forcing herself to lean over and kiss that ancient cheek.

"Nannie writes of you so often, my dear," said Aurelia. "I know you are your grandmother's shining star. And now you have a third backseat driver! You'll need strong character to combat us. As we proceed to the restaurant, would you be kind enough to bring my walker? Alas, I can go nowhere without it. It's quite the latest thing: hand brakes, seat, tote basket. You young people have your all-terrain vehicles, but I have my all-terrain walker."

This was not the conversation of a woman who had lost her marbles. Flo and Nannie were giddy with relief. They all but danced and clapped.

Brit looked around Room 217.

Rose was smiling at nothing.

Plain white walls were interrupted by plain white shades raised exactly halfway.

Odors of Clorox and cafeteria meals on trays wafted down the hall.

And all around was silence, thick and dusty, as if people were even too old and too sick for television.

Aston 3 had put Aurelia in this white coffin, this storage area for somebody who wasn't dead yet, as easily as someone might put a dog in a kennel for the weekend.

"Time to go!" shouted Flo. She shoved Aurelia into the wheelchair, whipped out the door and headed for the elevator.

Rose, however, wanted to chat. "Are you Mrs. Gibbs's older or younger sister?" she called after Flo.

One thing about being old and deaf: you could pick the questions you felt like answering and nobody could do anything about it. "Are you the only aide on duty today, Rose?" said Nannie, charging out the door after Flo. "My, what a hard worker you are!" she called over her shoulder.

"Sonya's on duty too," said Rose, "but we're responsible for the whole floor and it's run, run, run. Never a moment to relax."

Brit could see Sonya watching television in the nurses' station.

Rose thrust a clipboard into Brit's hands. Her third clipboard in two days. Normally you didn't see a clipboard for months at a time. It was a form requiring Visitor's name, address and phone number. "Alzheimer's patients are hard to keep track of," explained Rose with a shrug. "They get lost. And we send a copy of Mrs. Gibbs's visitor list to her son."

Brit dropped the clipboard into the wire basket of the walker and followed the girls. The walker didn't push easily and it didn't pull easily. She was halfway down the hall before she thought of checking for brakes.

"And of course now Dr. Gibbs is involved with Mrs. Gibbs's own doctor—Dr. White," Rose whispered confidentially. "Don't you think that's the sweetest most romantic thing?"

Nannie was right, thought Brit. He paid the doctor off. "And you have a front-row seat, Rose!" she said. "Tell me everything."

Flo was halfway to the elevator. Nannie was passing on the right, charging ahead to poke the Down button.

Rose giggled. "I think Dr. Gibbs comes to visit the doctor more than his mother. Isn't that cute?"

It's disgusting, thought Brit. "It's adorable!" she cried.

"I love to watch Dr. White and Dr. Gibbs hold hands. Once I caught them necking. My really old patients call it spooning; isn't that just the cutest word? He's so handsome, and I love his voice, like a commentator on BBC."

They caught up to the girls and stepped into the elevator, which crept back down.

"When do you think you'll be back?" Rose asked Brit.

Brit imitated her mother. "Why don't we play it by ear?" she said, using a phrase that never failed Mom. "Tell you what. I'll phone from the Red Lion after we've had our dessert and coffee."

When the elevator doors opened at the ground floor, Brit said she'd bring the car around. She ran ahead into the rain, which was clean and clear, washing away the smell of the ward. She fit Aurelia's walker in the back of the van and disposed of the clipboard under the lap blankets. Then she drove under the overhang of the front door, hopped out and positioned the crucial step stool. Rose helped Aurelia out of the wheelchair. "Goodness me," said Aurelia. "Brittany Anne, won't you please dash back and get my rain hat from the closet?"

"Aurelia, we don't have time for that," said Flo.

"And anything else you see that I might need, Brittany Anne," Aurelia added.

Aurelia needed everything. Talk about traveling light. She could hardly fit a second tissue into that tiny green bag.

"In the closet, Brittany Anne," said Aurelia. "Go up through the lobby, but be sure not to waste time coming down on that slow elevator. Use the back stairs next to my room. So much faster."

What was with the stair instruction? Brit bet neither Aurelia nor her walker had ever set foot on a stair. "Rain hat," she agreed. "I'm on it."

She and Rose rolled their eyes at each other and it didn't take acting on Brit's part.

★ ★ ★

There was no sign of Sonya.

Brit went into Aurelia's room and opened the closet door. It was small. Not a tenth of Brit's wardrobe could have hung here, and she hadn't had eighty-six years to collect shoes and handbags. It was weirdly empty. The only thing on the only shelf was the rain hat, one of those horrible pleated plastic bags old ladies tied under their chins and nobody even knew where they bought them. The closet floor was covered with odd bumpy white pillows. Brit looked inside a pillowcase. A pair of navy blue pumps stared back at her, and beneath them, sensible leather flats.

Aurelia Gibbs had packed for Maine.

I love this woman, thought Brit. She peeked out the door. No Sonya. She hoisted two pillowcases, stepped out of the room, opened the stair door and swung the pillowcases onto the landing. It hardly took a minute to toss the other five after them. She grabbed the rain hat, gave the room a last check and turned to find Sonya in the doorway.

"Hi!" said Brit. "Mrs. Gibbs forgot her rain hat."

"They always forget something, don't they?" said Sonya affectionately. "I called Dr. Gibbs. He wants to talk to you."

"Gosh!" said Brit, who had not said "gosh" since third grade. "I can't wait to talk to him. It's been ages!" She was terrified. Here she was, stealing both his mother and his mother's property, and he knew! She comforted herself with the thought that at least he couldn't possibly know her name or how to find her. "Isn't he just a doll?" she said to Sonya, feeling trapped and sick. "Don't you think he has a romantic voice like somebody from BBC television?"

"Oh, yes!" cried Sonya. "We all adore him."

"I'm hoping he'll marry Dr. White, aren't you?" said Brit.

Sonya clapped her hands and jumped up and down. "Has he said anything to the family?" she whispered.

"We pick up any clue we can."

"Us too!" cried Sonya. Her desk telephone began to ring. "I'll be right back," she promised.

Time to bail, thought Brit. Sonya trotted away; Brit took two silent steps after her, reached the stair door, turned the knob, hoped for the best, stepped inside and softly closed the door after her. Nobody ever raced up and down a flight of stairs faster or with more pillowcases.

When Sonya answered the phone, she'd look back, see nobody and figure that Brit was waiting in Aurelia's room. When she got off the phone and didn't find Brit in 217, she'd think Brit had taken the elevator to the lobby. If the phone call was long, Brit had a long time. If the phone call was short, she didn't.

On the ground floor, Brit peeked out onto grass and empty parking lots. The Safari would be around the corner, with Aurelia wondering whether Brit was smart enough to figure out what she was supposed to do and Rose wondering what was taking so long.

Dozens of windows faced Brit. Hoping the patients had bad eyes or were watching television, she put the pillowcases out on the grass, shut the door behind her and raced back to the car, where Rose was still fixing everybody's seat belt. When you were old, you could stall for time better than anybody.

"Hurry up, Brit!" yelled Flo. "We'll miss our reservation."

If Rose asked for her clipboard, what would Brit say? But Rose chatted about the van. "This is a nice spacious car, Brit. What kind is it, anyway?"

Brit could see how criminals who had just meant to rob a bank ended up shooting everybody. She was having homicidal feelings toward Rose. "It's a Beemer," said Brit, ready to add "Just kidding," in case Rose knew anything about cars. But it started to pour, and Rose, with the usual female fear of wet hair, scurried back inside.

Brit vaulted into the driver's seat and sped around the parking lots. Then she turned into a one-person relay race, heaving pillowcases in the pouring rain. Anybody looking out the window had quite a show. She hoped it wasn't Sonya.

She hefted the last pillowcase, turned too fast and lost her grip. The pillowcase skidded across the wet grass like a child on a water slide. From its open mouth poured bracelets and pendants, necklaces and rings, which skittered over the grass and hid under thick green turf. Brit dropped to her knees in the rain and began gathering gems. They looked real.

"What's wrong?" cried Nannie.

"I spilled all the jewelry!"

"The jewelry doesn't matter!" Aurelia called. "Brittany, we need to leave quickly! I feel sure they've phoned Aston by now. Aston will demand that they prevent me from going."

Brit loved jewelry. She wanted to design jewelry someday and have her own shop. She had no interest in precious stones, though. She liked crazy baubles and weird beads and bracelets of rusty rivets and pendants of blown glass and earrings of silk flowers. So she was amazed by how intensely she wanted these real gems. She couldn't leave them in the grass for lawn mowers to chop up. And the jewelry had mattered enough for Aurelia to pack it. She lifted a bracelet with two rows of diamonds—and every fifth stone an emerald. It was Tiffany-display-window beautiful.

A face appeared into a nearby window and stared at her.

"Now!" cried Aurelia. "Please!"

Brit shoved the bracelet into her pocket, grabbed the half-empty pillowcase, raced to the car and leaped into the driver's seat.

"Faster!" shrieked Flo.

"It's a nursing home!" Brit yelled back. "You think an armed janitor is going to vault off a balcony, land on the roof of the car and throw Aurelia back in bed?"

Nannie giggled.

Aurelia said, "Yes."

Flo shouted, "Turn right!"

Brit turned right. Fox Hills Adult Community was out of sight.

In moments, Sonya would be searching for her. The secretary would be saying Brit hadn't come back through the lobby. Sonya would be opening the closet door. Alarms would be raised. And somebody was going to find diamonds in the grass.

Brit made another turn and another, reached Route 7 again and turned south.

Second day of summer vacation. Brittany Anne Bowman was a kidnapper and a thief.

CHAPTER 7

"**T**ell us what happened when Aston put you in Fox Hills," said Flo.

"I fought back," said Aurelia. "I don't weigh a hundred pounds and I can hardly lift a paperback book, but I tried to hit them. They used straps to hold me down to the mattress. I lay there listening to my own son telling lies. How dearly he loved me, he kept saying. How it broke his heart to admit that his beloved mother was senile. After they strapped me down, he patted me, like upholstery. He listed ways in which I was failing and non compos mentis—not one of which was true!—and they believed him. *Everybody* believed him. He was flashing a piece of paper, which he insisted was a power of attorney. I never gave him a power of attorney. And then they medicated me."

High school was about getting ready to make each of your own decisions. A nursing home, then, was about surrendering each of your own decisions.

"When they lowered the dose and I could think again, I had no home, no friends and, for some time, not even a telephone. I lay waiting to die."

She lost her home, thought Brit, and her own kitchen and reading chair and friends—and even hope.

"And then, Nannie darling, your letter was forwarded. *Reunion is coming,* you wrote. And I decided to live."

Brit checked her rearview mirror, just in case the janitors *had* leaped into fast cars and were chasing them. But the road was empty. Actually this whole corner of Massachusetts was a little too empty for Brit.

"My son wishes I would just die," said Aurelia. "He's tired of having me around and getting in his way."

Nannie didn't like ugly stories (which cut way back on the TV programs she could watch), so she said, "Aston meant well. He felt he had no choice."

"Aston did not mean well!" snapped Aurelia. "He had plenty of choices."

Brit needed messages from people cheerier than Aurelia.

She threw her weight sideways while keeping the steering wheel steady. Lifting her thigh but not shifting her grip on the wheel, so she wouldn't end up in a ditch, she peeled her cell phone out of her tight jeans pocket. She couldn't quite reach the diamond-and-emerald bracelet at the bottom of the same pocket to hand it over to Aurelia. When she lowered herself, the car was wavering around the lane. She straightened out and double-checked the rearview mirror.

A police car was behind her.

No way! she thought. It's a mirage.

She looked a second time. Definitely a police car.

Brit could hardly hold on to the wheel.

The diamond-and-emerald bracelet felt very stolen.

Aurelia felt very kidnapped.

The Safari felt very illegal.

And that last little maneuver? Where she jittered all over the road trying to get her phone out? Not illegal, maybe, but not wise either. At least she hadn't *used* the phone.

She wanted to scream. The girls' chatter sounded like the yapping of little dogs.

Okay, calm down, she said to herself. His siren isn't on. His lights aren't flashing. Perhaps he was just there. Didn't police cruise their territories, eyes open for crime? Brit slowed way down and this totally annoyed the cop, who sped up, and now he was on top of her bumper.

Brit had never had a police car behind her. It was a hideous experience. If there had been a single store in all western Massachusetts with a single parking space, she would have pulled in and bought anything just so the cop would pass. Naturally she was surrounded by fields that were wet down to the center of the earth. If she drove off the road here, she'd sink to her hubcaps and the policeman would stay by her side and call the tow truck and there would be another clipboard and it would be revealed that she was illegally driving. One thing would lead to another, Aurelia would be strapped down on a fresh mattress and Aston 3 would gloat.

Having made a brief stand for being nice at all times, Nannie quit. "You are so right, Aurelia," said Nannie. "Aston Three is a goose end."

Brit forgot the cop.

Canada geese were all over the place all year long in Connecticut. You could not pretend that a goose powdered its nose. What came out the end of a goose were great green gobs that ruined playing fields, wrecked lawns, stained sneakers and disfigured parks. When Nannie called Aston 3 a goose end, she was calling him a shit.

Brit wanted to meet the man who was so awful that Nannie—out loud, in front of the girls—called him a shit.

The policeman was now all but touching her rear bumper. Brit decided to design a digital pop-up for car roofs so you could type in messages for other drivers. She had plenty to say to a cop who was terrifying her plus tailgating. No wonder people had road rage.

"Mass Pike east to Boston, Brittany Anne," said Aurelia. "We'll turn north at Worcester, however, because we are headed for Fitchburg. We should arrive with sufficient time to go to the thrift shop and the cemetery."

"The thrift shop?" said Brit. A woman who abandoned diamonds in the grass wanted to go to a thrift shop? Brit hated thrift shops. She hated anything used but especially used clothing. So what if you could put it through the wash? It still had somebody else's sweat on it. She even hated used books. Call them secondhand, call them antique—they were *used*.

Dad said Brit would have to earn a lot of money if she was opposed to anything secondhand. Mom said it was a moral advantage; Brit could become a hermit, having no possessions and reveling in the serenity of emptiness. Brit felt that the better solution was to earn tons of money so she could always buy new and always be shopping.

She put on her turn signal for the entrance ramp to the Mass Pike.

The policeman put on *his* signal for the entrance ramp to the Mass Pike.

Brit tried to stay calm. If he had planned to pull her over, he'd have done it by now. This had to be a coincidence, even though Brit was not a great believer in coincidence. She merged into traffic and the policeman ripped onto the highway, passed her without a glance and got into the fast lane. He accelerated and vanished over the horizon.

Brit was weak with relief. "What kind of a doctor is Aston Three anyway?" she yelled over her shoulder.

"A PhD doctor," said Flo. "He's a college professor and he doesn't earn much, but he lives well. Year after year, Aurelia shells out. She gives him great cars and great vacations and great divorces. How many divorces so far, Aurelia?"

"Four. Grad students find him attractive and there's always a lovely young thing adorning his life. But he doesn't marry them anymore, although he is pretending to the woman doctor who went along with his diagnosis of me as senile that they'll get married and have a baby."

A baby! thought Brit. That is disgusting. By the time this poor kid reaches high school, his father will be seventy-five. Or dead. "Dr. White," she said. "Rose was telling me. She thinks it's very romantic."

"It's horrid," said Aurelia. "Dr. White is forty-one and is willing to do anything for a baby. Aston is fifty-nine and willing to do anything for my money."

That was enough about middle age for Brit. She could believe she would one day be in college and she could believe she would one day have a wedding; in fact, wedding plans were one of her favorite hobbies. But she could not picture beyond her twenty-first or twenty-second birthday, and even that was her at sixteen, only older.

She turned her cell phone on.

FIRST NEW VOICE MESSAGE:

"Darling, what is going on? I'm feeling a high degree of tension. We can't reach you at Nannie's, your cell phone is off, and Lindsay Dorrelle has left a message about the police. Call immediately and let your father and me know what is happening."

SECOND NEW VOICE MESSAGE:

"Did they catch you? Call and tell me how it went. I'm still here in the rain being bored and you're crossing state lines with kidnap victims. Don't forget that's when they call the FBI and you end up in federal prison instead of local jail. I can't drive up and bail you out because I don't drive and I'm broke. Call and let me know what's happening."

THIRD NEW VOICE MESSAGE:

"You never called me back so probably you were too much of a coward to telephone Coop and you don't want to admit it, and I won't hear from you again until you've had a reunion with a thousand creaky old hags in Maine. If we're really friends, you'll text me at Dairy Queen."

FOURTH NEW VOICE MESSAGE:

"Brittany, it's your father. We were too worried to get on the launch and look for sea lions. Where are you? *What is happening?*"

Brit slammed on the brakes and pulled into the breakdown lane.

"What's wrong?" cried the girls in a chorus.

"Just sit there!" yelled Brit. She hit Dad's cell number. He picked up on the first ring. She imagined him sitting on the edge of his king-sized bed in Alaska, waiting for her call. "Hi, Dad! I'm totally sorry you got worried. Nannie accidentally turned off the ringer on her phones and that's why we didn't hear you, and Lindsay's version of what happened? She's wrong. See, Hayley drove over and we practiced backing up and parallel parking and forgot how soft the ground is from all this rain and left tire tracks and it's my fault and I'm calling a landscape crew and they're coming to fix it and I'll even pay for it! And Lindsay Dorrelle did call the police, which I will never forgive, so take her off our Christmas card list."

Dad fell for it. That's what you got when you trusted your kid; sometimes you were wrong. Mom required more details, but she fell for it too. The only iffy part was when Mom wanted to speak to Nannie. "Oh, dear," said Brit, "she's napping. You were right, Mom, Nannie is failing a tiny bit."

Nannie stuck out her tongue.

As soon as Brit disconnected, the girls got on her case for saying Nannie was failing. "You guys have been lying to authority all day," said Brit, making a note to tell Hayley her share of the front yard destruction. This would be a true test of friendship. "It was my turn to fib. Now there's something I need to ask, Aurelia. How would you have gotten those pillowcases out of the building without me?"

"I wouldn't have, dear. I had expected to leave without anything, but when Nannie phoned last night and told me you were driving, I saw that I could use you."

Everybody was using her: Coop to solve his boredom, Aurelia to carry her luggage, Nannie to do her driving. Even her parents were just using her to babysit Nannie.

"As long as you're on the phone, darling," said Nannie, "telephone the Red Lion Inn and cancel our lunch reservation."

Brit called information and got the number and called the inn and canceled lunch, and Flo said, "Add my cell phone number to your phone address book, in case we get separated."

Like how are we going to get separated, Brit wanted to know, when you guys can't move without me?

"We had a nice room at the inn last night, didn't we?" said Flo. "The shower was easy to get into. Sometimes they have these high tubs and you can't step over the edge, or if you do get over the edge, you fall and break your neck. Where are we staying tonight, Aurelia?"

"The Sheraton in Fitchburg, adjacent to my attorney's office."

"Can Aston find us there?" asked Nannie.

"He can't possibly know what I'm up to. And he would never think of the Sheraton, because when I'm in the area, I don't stay in a hotel. My summer house is just up the road in Ashburnham."

None of this meant a thing to Brit. She went back to the crucial part. "What does a thrift shop have to do with anything?"

"After he kidnapped me," said Aurelia, "Aston hijacked my possessions."

"Aurelia," said Flo irritably, "you can write a new will, and we can witness it, but Aston will contest it even before you're dead. He will claim you're a dotty old bag who can't write a grocery list, never mind a will. If you use words like *kidnap* and *hijack* when your dear son, beloved by all, has taken proper care of you in a fine institution, the judge will agree that you are exhibiting the paranoia common to Alzheimer's patients."

There was a pause.

Lush green hills went by.

"In rational terms, then," said Aurelia, "Aston sold my house in Wellesley for a million six hundred thousand dollars and auctioned off the contents. He didn't care about the crystal, which was a wedding gift to my grandmother, or the quilt stitched by my older sister, who died of diphtheria. He cared only for the money. He even referred to my possessions as the estate, as if I were already dead. Not one penny of that sale came back to me."

Aston had a million six hundred thousand dollars plus what he raked in from antique auctions? And *still* he needed money? Maybe he ran down to the Indian casinos in Connecticut every weekend and lost. Or maybe he and Dr. White *were* getting married and wanted a waterfront mansion in a trendy town.

"You see, Brittany, I also own the farmhouse in which I grew up, in the little village of Ashburnham, outside of Fitchburg." Aurelia's voice drifted into storytelling mode. "The farmhouse is plain, with plain old rooms and plain old barns. The kitchen had a deep cast-iron sink and a big white stove on six legs. My dogs liked to sleep under the stove because it was cozy and safe, especially during thunderstorms. We did laundry in the cellar. I didn't like that cellar. I was afraid of catching my fingers in the mangle. My grandmother loved to can, so the shelves along the cellar stairs were lined with jars of watermelon relish and her best applesauce."

Brit checked the speedometer. She was speeding. So was everybody else, but everybody else wasn't a kidnapper. She set her cruise control at sixty-five and removed her foot from the accelerator. It was kind of too bad the state police weren't after them. Two days of this and she felt more than competent to handle fast turns and speedy exits. Mentally she played her favorite footage from *The*

French Connection, in which they barely missed mowing down baby carriages as they screamed through intersections.

"Aston sold the contents of the farmhouse," said Aurelia, "but the house itself has not yet sold. It's sitting there, vacant and uncared for. A house without heat deteriorates quickly, you know. An antique shop picked the place over for agricultural implements and kitchen artifacts. Whatever they didn't want was sent to a thrift shop in Fitchburg."

"But Aurelia," said Nannie, "it was November when Aston put you in Fox Hills, and January or February, say, when he cleared out the farmhouse. It's June. How could anything still be at the thrift shop?"

"Some things are slow to sell," said Aurelia defiantly.

"What exactly might be that slow to sell?" Flo asked.

Brit watched Aurelia in the mirror. Buttermeres, she thought, never surrender. They kidnap, they lie, they scout out thrift shops.

"My wedding gown," said Aurelia Gibbs. "I had it in a box in the attic under a pile of old tablecloths and I am hopeful that the entire box went to the thrift shop."

Her kid sold his mother's *wedding gown?*

Brit's phone, lying on the passenger seat for ready reference, started to ring. She picked it up, hoping it would be Coop. Okay, fine, he was using her, but it *was* fine; she wanted to be used if it was Coop. Admit it, she said to herself, any connection with Cooper James is a good one.

But it was not Coop.

DR. ASTON ANDREW GIBBS III said the screen. Brit had not thought of him with Roman numerals. So he was Aston III, not Aston 3.

How could he know who she was? How could he have her cell

phone number? Her hands got slippery on the wheel. Her eyes flicked to the rearview mirror. There were a lot of cars on the highway, and suddenly, everything in sight, both directions, seemed small and low to the ground except her. Her Safari was high and bronze and very visible. Was Aston in one of these little cars? Would he pull up next to her and stare through the window?

She turned the heat up and aimed a vent at herself. Rose couldn't have identified the Safari, she told herself. She thinks it's a BMW. And she didn't write down the license number. *I feel* exposed, but actually, I'm anonymous.

None of the girls had heard the phone ring. "Aurelia, you didn't have a wedding when you married Aston Gibbs Junior," said Flo. "You went to a justice of the peace. We were there. You wore a pale pink suit with a triple rope of pearls."

"My wedding," said Aurelia, "to Woollie."

The trucks on the Mass Pike seemed larger and faster. The rain seemed harder and darker. "Who's Woollie?" asked Brit. Aston had left a voice message. What should she do about it? Aurelia didn't want to talk to him; she hated him and he had lied about the power of attorney, whatever that was. *Brit* wasn't about to chat with Aston. What was he, Superman, that he knew her cell phone number? The girls were settling in happily to hear Aurelia's story. How could Brit fling Aston into their faces?

"Ashburnham was so isolated and tiny it did not have a public high school. The centerpiece of the village is a boarding school, and we townies went as day students. My best friend was my classmate Woollston Chandler. Woollie and I rode ponies and bicycles and shared litters of puppies. We went fishing and explored the woods but when I turned thirteen my mother

94

insisted that I behave like a lady. I saw less of Woollie, because it takes a lot of time and laundry to be a lady. We did go to church together and play tennis together and one day we were walking home from school and I said, 'Woollie, could you ever love me?' and he said, 'I've *always* loved you, Aurelia. I'm yours.' And we kissed. Not the kisses in movies today, aggressive attack kissing. Ours was gentle and long and almost chaste."

"I've never had any use for chaste kisses," said Flo.

Aurelia paid no attention. Brit thought this might have been the case for sixty-five years. "I attended college in Maine," said Aurelia, "while Woollie went to Harvard. When Woollie drove up to see me, he'd squire all the girls, and if Florence or Nannie or Daisy had a boyfriend at the moment, that boy would come along too."

"What do you mean, '*if*'?" said Flo crossly. "I've always had a boyfriend at the moment."

"Do you have one now?" said Nannie eagerly.

Aurelia raised her voice. "When Woollie and I were married, I wore a white gown with seed pearls sewn on by Woollie's grandmother. It took her months. Do they study World War Two anymore, Brittany?"

Brit didn't care about war; she wanted to know the style of the gown and whether Flo had a boyfriend.

"The Depression hit my generation hard, and before any of us realized what was happening, the Second World War hit us too. Woollie enlisted, of course. I was so proud of him. I'm still proud of him. But I wish he had come home again. He was killed March 8, 1942."

So that was why they were hitting both a thrift shop and a cemetery. This would be a two-tombstone week.

Brit's phone rang again. The girls didn't hear it this time

either. Brit reminded herself that it was not a crime to leave a phone unanswered. But her mouth got dry and her heart pounded a little too fast.

"A year after I was widowed," said Aurelia, "a fine young man, Aston Gibbs Junior, proposed to me. Back then you could hardly imagine life without marriage. I couldn't remain a widow. An unmarried woman was a lesser thing. I didn't love Aston the way I loved Woollie, but I was fond of him."

Brit registered a prayer with God. It's okay about the state troopers, she told Him. I'll handle them. But don't let me be "fond" of my husband. Let me love him with all my heart and body, and don't let him get killed young.

Every girl on earth would have the same list. God must be caught in an avalanche of demands for love. But my love really matters, she said to God. Put my love at the top.

"I did not let go of Woollie in my heart," said Aurelia. "I know it was a sin. I kept my wedding gown in the farmhouse attic. Every year on our anniversary, I would travel alone to the farmhouse and wear it. Then I would read Woollie's letters. He didn't write many. He hated writing. *Dear Aurelia,* he would write from the front. He was in the Pacific. *I miss you so. Home soon. Love, Woollie.* Then I didn't get any more letters. I got a telegram."

Brit wept for them all, even Aston junior, the husband who was second best his whole marriage and didn't know. Or had he known? That would be hard.

"Here's a hanky, Brittany," said Aurelia. "I always keep a spare tucked in my sleeve." Flo passed up a crisply ironed lace-edged white handkerchief. *Somebody* at Fox Hills was nice, because somebody was ironing for Aurelia.

"Woollie was one of the boys you knew wouldn't die when he marched off to war," said Nannie. "He was too good for dying."

"If only," said Flo sadly, "there was a law that kept the good ones alive."

Yet another topic to leave in the hands of eighty-six-year-olds. Brit gathered her courage, flicked her phone open and listened to her first message.

"This is Dr. Aston Gibbs. I've talked to the staff at the Red Lion Inn."

Mystery solved. The Red Lion Inn had caller ID.

"My mother needs constant supervision. She does not have her medications with her because the nurses keep all pharmaceuticals. I know you don't mean to do this, Ms. Bowman, but taking her out of Fox Hills is dangerous. Please call me back right now. My mother gets confused and angry. No doubt she's misled you. I'm so sorry you were drawn into this."

Brit's heart sank. He had a nice voice. He sounded like a nice man.

SECOND NEW VOICE MESSAGE:

"Please, Ms. Bowman. You've got to call me back. In case you can't talk to me, let me give you her physician's phone number. Dr. White can give you some facts about Alzheimer's. Patients with this terrible disease can be pathological liars. My mother needs her medications in specific doses at specific times. You are endangering her life." He sounded exhausted, facing yet another crummy situation involving his elderly mother. He sounded loving.

The girls were still talking about Woollie. They did not know him dead; they knew him as an athlete eager to paddle a canoe, as a boyfriend eager to dance a tango.

Brit needed a second opinion. And not from somebody eighty-six. She called Hayley, but Hayley didn't pick up; she probably had DQ customers. Brit called Coop.

"What stage are you at?" asked Coop.

"Postkidnap blues," she said. The girls nattered on, not even aware that Brit was having her own conversation in the front seat. "I'm wondering if I did the right thing."

"Probably not," said Coop. "Catch me up."

She caught him up. "The question is . . . do I call Aston back? If I call him, Nannie hates me, Aurelia goes back to prison, there's no sixty-fifth reunion, and no new will."

"But if you don't call Aston back, what about this medicine Aurelia has to take?"

"I don't know," said Brit gloomily. "My mother said that Aurelia was on about a hundred medications and that's why her son had to put her in a nursing home. Do you happen to know what a power of attorney is?"

"A legal instrument. It gives somebody else the power to sign documents for you and make your decisions. If Aston has one, he can sell her house and anything else because Aurelia set it up that way."

"How do you know?"

"TV. I watch anything forensic or law enforcement or emergency room or cop or FBI or autopsy. If the power of attorney doesn't exist, though, Aurelia could probably get Aston arrested for stealing."

"He's her son. She probably doesn't want to arrest him. She probably still loves him even though she hates him."

"Yeah. I always felt that way about Rupert," said Coop. "You know what? Rupert was always having to get a lawyer. You guys are seeing a lawyer in the morning. Put this all on the lawyer. Let him decide. Meanwhile, do *you* think Aurelia's senile?"

"Don't use that word. It's disgusting. It means *old, useless, dated, ought to be dead by now.* No. I don't."

"Ask her about those medications and whether she needs them to stay coherent. Or even alive."

"I don't want to be rude, Coop."

"Kidnappers have passed through rude into heavier stuff, Brit."

She giggled. What was Coop doing right now? Where was he sitting and what was he wearing? She pictured him in sweat-pants and no shirt, on an old sofa, staring at a TV on mute, a dog asleep on his feet.

It had been a bad decision to put the car on cruise control, because she had almost stopped driving. She was letting the car drive—just what her mother had feared, except it wasn't Nannie who had forgotten to steer. "Later, Coop!" She got back in an actual lane and yelled, "Aurelia! What about your medications?"

"You are so thoughtful to be concerned, Brittany Anne," said Aurelia. "After Aston kidnapped me, my former next-door neighbor mailed every bottle and jar of pills to me, and nobody at Fox Hills knows that I have my own supply. Last night I transferred my stash into my little silk handbag. The supply will last until I get to a real doctor again. Now, keep your eyes open for a good shopping mall," she instructed. "Preferably with Filene's as the anchor. I cannot appear at my sixty-fifth college reunion hauling my possessions in frayed pillowcases. I require decent luggage. Most people, Brittany Anne, attend a reunion every five or ten years. We girls attend annually and we are celebrities on campus. We will be photographed and interviewed all week long because we come back every year."

"Because we're alive *at all*," Flo corrected.

Brit looked at her watch. Watches were sensible things that didn't shoot from the topic of wedding gowns to war or from doctors who ought to lose their licenses to department stores. Watches stuck to their specialty. It was exactly one p.m.

Considering that they had already kidnapped somebody and driven halfway across Massachusetts, this was just amazing.

Brit's phone rang.

She didn't answer. She drove half a mile. Then she checked her messages.

"You're not giving me a choice, Ms. Bowman. I have to alert the state police. Call me now or I call them."

CHAPTER 8

Every girl's favorite summer vacation: wanted by the police.

She could not imagine being pulled over. Police—armed—slowly, threateningly walking up to her.

Her thoughts were racing faster than any car on the road.

First of all, she told herself, Aurelia is a grown-up. She does get to decide where she lives. She's decided not to live at Fox Hills. There's no crime in it, for her or for me. So big deal, we fibbed to a hospital aide about where we were having lunch.

What could Aston say to the cops if he called them? He certainly couldn't say "I'm afraid she'll change her will."

He couldn't say "I forged her signature on a power of attorney and stole her money."

But he *could* say "I'm worried because she doesn't have her medications."

Would the police chase Aurelia down for that? Brit thought they would. She was not an anti-police kind of teenager. She didn't want them in her yard, examining her rosebushes, and she didn't want them in her life, examining her driver's license, but overall, she did want police.

The problem with police was, sometimes they wanted to be cowboys.

Her stomach quivered at the thought of being chased and hunted.

But I, she reminded herself, am not an old lady. And from now on, I refuse to drive like one either. I'll be the cowboy, thank you.

She clicked off cruise control and went as fast as everybody else. It was nice not to be passed by every vehicle in Massachusetts.

Okay. So. Aston—a guy busily selling antiques, dating doctors and spending a million six hundred thousand. Would he also drive all over Massachusetts on the off chance he might bump into his mother?

If for any reason the van got pulled over and Aston actually *had* reported that a girl in a GMC Safari . . .

Brit giggled. Perhaps Rose would tell him it was a Beemer.

Behind her, the girls had slid into stories about college and the Depression. They talked about malted milk shakes and Shirley Temple movies and the shocking moment when Rhett Butler said a swear word at the end of *Gone With the Wind*. Flo had the way back; Aurelia and Nannie were in the middle. Flo was leaning forward and Nannie was sitting sideways so they could both face Aurelia, who was not flexible. They were laughing and interrupting and holding hands.

The girls were almost having Reunion here in the car, but real Reunion had requirements. They had to check in at Buttermere Dormitory, get their class badges, be photographed on the steps, sing their alumnae song.

Brit could not treat the girls like children again. She had to tell them about Aston's threats. But even when there was a lull in the flow of memories, Brit couldn't launch the awful topic of Aston, so she said, "What does Buttermere look like? All I know are the front steps from that photograph."

"It's been torn down," said Flo.

"It couldn't be remodeled to meet building codes," explained Nannie. "We outlived it."

They've outlived everything, Brit thought. Parents, husbands, some of their children, their health, parts of their minds and even their buildings. I'm not telling them about Aston. Let them dream of Reunion, not recapture. Anyway, I bet Aston won't really do anything except sputter.

She turned north on I-290 and forty-five minutes later, they arrived in Fitchburg.

"A sad little city," said Aurelia. "It lacks charm, jobs, shops and good schools."

Brit giggled. "But it has a Friendly's," she said, pointing, "so let's have lunch." Friendly's had the slowest service in America and was therefore perfect for old ladies, who were the slowest customers in America.

The rain had dwindled to mist, but the girls wanted raincoats and rain hats because wet hair would be the death of them. In the awkward confines of the van, Brit helped everybody coat up. She moved Aurelia safely onto the footstool and got her upright between the handles of her walker, then herded the girls into the restaurant. When everybody had powdered their noses, she secured a booth, because Nannie loved booths. Flo and Nannie slid (with difficulty) to inside positions while Brit arranged Aurelia and her ATW on the outside. Since it would be approximately forever before lunch arrived, Brit headed back to the car.

First she called Mom and Dad, to assure them that everything was just peachy. She listened without listening to descriptions of Alaskan flora and fauna.

Coop had texted: me - classic baseball. u. - classic adventure.

Brit was feeling strong. Maybe it was shrugging about the police. Maybe it was driving on all these highways. She had too much to say for a text message and guts enough to phone. "So how come you're so friendly all of a sudden?" she started when Coop picked up.

"I did have to work up to it."

"For six months?"

"It threw me off."

"What threw you off? Trespassing on somebody else's personal private computer?"

"It was sitting there open. I saw a file with my name."

"Okay, so that was stupid, but it was a crush. Everybody has crushes."

"For a week, maybe, everybody has crushes. You started a file on me in seventh grade and kept it going. That's, like, years."

Brit felt they had covered this topic sufficiently. It was time for Cooper to feel humiliated instead. "So how come you can't drive at all ever? Can't you get a license without parental permission?"

"Sure. But what car would you like me to drive? Since it won't be my parents' car. And who might be paying the insurance, since it won't be them?"

Brit laughed. "I have to go. Nannie is waving from her booth."

"Okay, but what is Aston's full name? I love looking people up online. I'll find some dirt on him."

Brit bounced into Friendly's, feeling indeed pretty friendly toward the world. She had talked her way out of her ghastly past. Coop was being normal with her. In fact, he was being way beyond normal. He was being totally pleasant.

Nannie and Flo were discussing dyeing their hair. Nannie never had; Flo always had. Aurelia ignored them. "I need to buy luggage, Brittany Anne."

"There's a Marshalls in this strip mall. They won't have the best-quality luggage, but you don't need—" She almost said, "You don't need it to last very long, since you're so old," but she caught herself.

Aurelia frowned. "A tawdry discount store?"

Brit was offended. "I love Marshalls. And if we luck out and buy luggage, you guys can spend a happy evening in the hotel transferring things from pillowcases."

Aurelia brightened. She opened her tiny bag, which contained not only her pills and another neatly folded pressed hanky, but also a vial of Youth-Dew. She daubed herself in preparation for shopping. "I can't believe you wear Madonna's perfume," said Brit.

"Who?" said Aurelia. "Joan Crawford and Gloria Swanson wore Youth-Dew."

"Gloria Swanson wore Joy," Flo corrected her.

They were still arguing about perfume and dead actresses when Brit steered them into Marshalls.

While Aurelia tested zippers, Brit flew around the store, madly gathering underwear, tops, conditioner and a really cute pair of sandals in case it ever got warm, and still beat the girls to the cash register. Aurelia had four suitcases in tan and black, not top-of-the-line but not cheap either. A saleswoman carried them to the cash register and Aurelia handed over her credit card.

"I'm sorry, ma'am," the clerk told Aurelia. "Your credit card has been rejected."

"*My* card? Try it again, please."

But it still didn't get accepted. Brit called the customer assistance number on the back of Aurelia's card. "Bad news," she told Aurelia. "Their records show that your credit card was canceled last November."

Silently, Flo put the luggage on her own credit card.

It was pouring again. The manager carried the new luggage out to the Safari while Brit boosted the girls in. "Aston canceled my credit cards?" cried Aurelia. "He didn't think I'd ever shop again? Ever get new earrings? Have my hair styled? Buy a ticket to anything? You cancel a person's credit after she dies!"

Brit did not possess a credit card. Her friends had credit cards and debit cards. Brit ached for the time when she too could whip out a piece of plastic. After a driver's license—maybe even *before* a driver's license—it was the most adult thing she could think of.

Brit saw her life as a ladder: first boyfriend, first job, first credit card, first college tour. As fast as I climb into adulthood, she thought, the girls are shoved away—plastic rectangle by plastic rectangle.

Aurelia blotted her tears on a handkerchief that hadn't dried out from the last sobbing.

High in the air, across parking lots and distant roads, Brit spotted the sign for the Sheraton. She turned on the engine and headed toward their hotel.

"Florence?" said Aurelia in a defeated voice. "Might I use your portable telephone instrument?"

Flo was the kind of woman who seized on every appliance, tool, technology and entertainment the day it appeared, and upgraded at every delightful opportunity, whereas Aurelia and Nannie were the kind of women who continued to lead the life their parents had, and were dragged only by necessity or grandchildren into the twenty-first century. Nannie's first cell phone call had been the day before, and Aurelia's first was probably right now.

Whoever Aurelia was calling, she knew the number by heart.

Brit crossed Route 12 and entered a frontage road, bumping over railroad tracks and passing office buildings. The Sheraton was off to the right, with vast parking lots between it and the big-box stores in the distance.

"Aston, this is your mother," said Aurelia.

Oh, no! thought Brit. I should have told her he's called three times.

"You canceled my credit cards," said Aurelia. "I am not dead, Aston. I make my own financial decisions."

Brit went slowly through a deep puddle. This would be a lousy time to get bogged down.

"How I dispose of my jewelry is my concern. I am going to my reunion," said Aurelia quietly, "and I am not returning to Fox Hills." She disconnected. "Brittany Anne, if you will, please, check us into the Sheraton, so that our rooms are assured. However, I prefer not to waste precious time dragging luggage up. I want to visit Woollie's grave before I run out of strength."

Until the day before, Brit had not visited a grave. She wasn't acquainted with any dead people, whereas the girls were almost exclusively acquainted with dead people.

Since they were using Flo's credit card now, Flo and Brit went into the hotel and got four rooms in a row, because everybody wanted her own bathroom. Especially Brit.

"Smoking or non?" asked the clerk.

"Non," said Flo. "I used to smoke," she told Brit. "I adored cigarettes. I still adore cigarettes. I just don't smoke them."

Brit entertained herself with the hotel registration form. She listed Cadillac as the make of her car and ILVCP as her plate number.

"Do they still study Shakespeare in school?" Flo wanted to know. "Have you read your *King Lear*?"

Brit was exhausted by the eighty-six-year-old-ness of the girls. The way they changed their topics—and the topics they changed to! Yes, she'd studied *King Lear* and hated every line of it. It was hard to understand and ugly when you did. How come they never read stuff where everybody lived happily ever after?

She could live happily ever after with Cooper James. Even happily for a weekend. At least go to a movie together.

I'm such a girl, she thought. For Coop, this is rainy-day filler;

it won't lead anywhere, any more than watching cartoons leads somewhere. But for me . . .

"Shakespeare is always right," said Flo. "You don't grasp that when you're young. *How sharper than a serpent's tooth it is to have a thankless child.* Aurelia and King Lear gave their children everything. 'Here,' they said, thinking they were doing the right thing. 'Take my kingdom, my gold, my heart.' But it never works. The parent is left with nothing."

"You guys keep weighing me down with this stuff," said Brit, "I'm going to need a walker of my own."

"Or friends," said Flo.

En route to the cemetery, Brit managed her first rotary, a Massachusetts traffic circle around which cars rushed, trying to rip off your fender. You leaped into it like jump rope and had to burst out right where everybody else was speeding in. Brit went around this potential demolition derby twice before Flo screamed, "Just go! You have the right of way!"

Fine! Brit just went.

Drivers with different points of view honked and shook their fists, but she survived. She drove under railroad tracks, went around blind curves and narrowly missed little boys on little bikes playing in the road.

"We locals pronounce the name of our town *ASH-burn-ham*," said Aurelia, "but when Lord and Lady Ashburnham came from England for the bicentennial, they said *Ash BURN'm*."

Brit always bought *People* magazine when it featured anybody

English with a title. She hoped to snag a royal one day. She herself might have behaved stupidly once or twice, but the royals behaved stupidly all the time, and with her guidance, the princes might escape the family tendency.

"What were Lord and Lady Ashburnham like?" Flo asked. "Elegant? Regal?"

"I can't remember," said Aurelia.

The girls seized on the topic of Things I Used to Know but Couldn't Dredge up Now If My Life Depended on It. This reminded Brit. "Nannie! You forgot your macaroons, peanut brittle and pound cake!"

"You can keep your macaroons," said Flo. "But if Nannie made her famous chocolate pound cake, pass it here."

There were the distinctive sounds of Tupperware being popped open.

"I'll have some of the chocolate pound cake," called Brit.

"I don't share," Flo told her.

"Florence!" said Aurelia.

"Oh, all right." Flo tore off a chunk for Brit.

If we were both sixteen, we'd be best friends, thought Brit, using her jeans for a napkin.

They entered Ashburnham.

"It's a pleasant little place," said Flo doubtfully.

The boarding school campus was deserted at this time of year. No construction, no student tours, no dogs, no lawn mowers. Aurelia directed Brit up a lane so steep it felt as if the pavement would peel off. The narrow road curled around gravestones and ducked under tree branches. With every round, they got higher and saw more graves.

All the ancestors of Ashburnham, thought Brit, looking down

forever on the students. It was comforting, as if a great-uncle or second cousin might be supervising from the sky.

After weeks of rain, the ground was as soft as a mattress. Flo and Nannie walked carefully, shoes sinking into the grass. Aurelia rolled bumpily beside them.

Woollie's grave was a thin plain stone. WOOLLSTON CHANDLER, said the chiseled letters, BELOVED HUSBAND OF AURELIA.

On the road below—the only exit and only entrance to the hilltop cemetery—a small black car idled. From this angle, Brit could not identify it. The driver rolled his window down. He wore sunglasses. Two dark holes stared up at Brit.

"I won't lie here," said Aurelia sadly. "I'll be buried next to Aston junior. He ordered his own tombstone and engraved both our names on it. All my side needs is the second date."

Way back when Brit wondered what an eighty-six-year-old dreamed of, she had not considered a silent tombstone, waiting for a date of death.

The black car inched forward, half hidden now by tree branches and gravestones.

Brit took her phone out of her pocket. She hit Zoom and focused the camera on the driver, but he was too far away. It's not Aston, she told herself. It's somebody else with a perfectly good reason to park at the bottom of a cemetery and stare at us.

But the morning before, Nannie had said that Aston wanted Aurelia to hurry up and die. What if it was true? If Aston had driven eighty miles an hour while Brit was tootling around at sixty-five, plus Friendly's and Marshalls, he could have gotten here ages ago. He could be down there waiting for them. Planning to fill in the second date on the tombstone.

"We have to go," said Brit roughly. "Everybody in the car."

"Darling, don't be upset," said Nannie. "Death comes to us all."

Brit could not stand to hear Nannie talk as if death were sitting on the sofa. She suddenly saw her grandmother the way a stranger would see her: an old, old lady, her face so wrinkled it could have been shirred fabric. Nannie looked older than Flo, even older than Aurelia. *No*, thought Brit. "Everybody in the car! *Now.*"

But they were not the right age for hurrying and it was not the right surface. The one to fall was Flo.

Brit flung herself down next to Flo, thinking, She'll break her back on a tombstone edge and somersault down the hill.

"I'm all right," said Flo, gasping for breath. "The grass cushioned me. But I'm down."

Flo's muscles were not going to lift her body. Flo was stuck on the ground.

Brit got on all fours next to Flo, who used her for a brace and struggled to an undignified doggy-crawl position. Brit helped her straighten to a kneeling position, and then Brit hoisted and Flo staggered, and on the fourth try, Flo was on her feet. "I hate being *old*!" she cried. "I'm just a *carcass*."

Brit was starting to think she didn't want to live to a great old age. There were serious drawbacks.

The girls were now so nervous that Brit had to wheel Aurelia over the hillocks of grass and help her onto the footstool and into the van and then go back for Nannie and Flo, supporting one on each arm.

If the guy with the sunglasses meant them any harm, he had missed an easy chance.

She drove downhill because there was no place else to drive. The girls discussed hot water bottles and electric heating pads to put on Flo's bruises when they reached the Sheraton.

The campus was silent and empty.

There was no black car.

"We'll return to the Sheraton by another route," said Aurelia.

Had Aurelia noticed the black car? Did she too think they'd better shake it off?

"Turn left on Williams Road, Brittany Anne. We'll stop at my farmhouse."

Oh, please, it was just another detour. Brit was sick of detours. She wanted the day to end. Who cared about some old farmhouse with no furniture and no television and not even any applesauce on the cellar shelves?

She checked the rearview mirror for black cars.

Aurelia pointed to faint tracks in grass that hadn't been cut for so long it was lying down like wet hair. Little maple trees grew in the gutters of a sad little white house. An old well pump rusted by a side door.

Brit didn't want to drive in. The grass looked as if it could wind around the axle and trap her. She idled in the road while Aurelia drank in the sight of her childhood home.

It came to Brit that she had misunderstood this entire trip. This journey was not about Reunion. It was about saying good-bye.

The girls were saying good-bye to each other, to the wonderful sunny days when they were Buttermere girls. Good-bye to cemeteries where loved ones lay. Good-bye to a house where memories clung.

They would not pass this way again.

Maybe it was the weather, maybe it was Fitchburg, but there were enough empty parking spaces that even Brit could parallel park.

"Brittany Anne, perhaps you could go into the thrift shop for me," suggested Aurelia. "We're tired," she added, which was certainly true, because Nannie and Flo were asleep on Flo's special pillows.

In the thrift shop was a volunteer who looked just like Nannie except twenty years younger. Which was still pretty old.

"In November?" said Brit. "Maybe December or January? Did you get an old wedding gown with seed pearls?"

"We did," said the volunteer, beaming. "It should have gone to a museum. It sold the same morning to a young woman who was getting married but was so broke, she didn't even plan to have a gown. We buttoned her up in that lovely old dress and she was beautiful. She had only thirty dollars, which she needed to spend on kitchenware. We figured, what is a thrift shop for if not thrift? We sold it to her for five dollars."

Five dollars for the gown Woollie's grandmother had made by hand.

Back in the Safari, there was no way to be gentle. "It sold the day it came in, Aurelia."

Aurelia put her handkerchief over her face.

"You knew that would probably be the case," Flo said to her.

"Probably isn't knowing. Probably is still hoping."

Brit turned onto the same frontage road and bumped over the same railroad tracks. The offices were emptying out, and people were scuttling to their cars, hunched under umbrellas. Any day Brit would rather get wet than lug an umbrella. She couldn't wait to get out of her disgusting two-day-old clothes and stand in the shower and have some more chocolate pound cake and cut the price tags off her new clothes and see if anything fit.

In the turnaround of the Sheraton sat two police cars.

CHAPTER 9

The police vehicles—engines running, doors open, radios on—were blocking the entrance to the hotel. Brit took her foot off the gas. The Safari came to a halt in a no-man's-land of parking spaces and scrawny trees in little parking lot gardens.

"There's something I should have told you," said Brit. "Aston got my cell phone number from when I called the Red Lion. He's left three messages. He said he'd call the police if I didn't call him back and give you up, Aurelia."

The girls studied the police cars.

Aurelia shook her head. "Rationally, I do not think policemen parked at a hotel in Fitchburg have anything to do with us. I expect some unpleasant guest has raised a ruckus or refused to pay a portion of his bill."

"Irrationally, though?" asked Nannie.

"They're after us," agreed Flo. She whipped out her cell phone. Unfolding her copy of the hotel registration, she dialed the Sheraton. "Good evening. This is Mrs. Heff. I booked rooms a little while ago."

Brit, Nannie and Aurelia leaned close to the phone.

"Yes, ma'am?" said the Sheraton.

"We're driving on to Boston instead," said Flo. "We're practically there already. I need to cancel. We never went into our rooms and didn't even pick up our keys, let alone use the sheets or towels, so you won't bill me, will you? I hate paying for something I didn't use." Flo was having a grand time. Brit could totally see her on that college campus, sneaking out of Buttermere Dormitory for Young Ladies, creeping around the bushes with Nannie and Daisy in tow, jimmying a window in the dining hall, sliding through into the basement kitchen and handing out a tray of baloney sandwiches.

"Wait!" cried the clerk. "Stay on the line, will you?"

"Thank you so much!" cried Flo, hanging up. She said to the girls, "They'll have caller ID at the Sheraton too. Bet a hundred dollars they'll call back in one minute."

Brit backed into a slot from which they could study police action but be shielded from view by heavy-leafed trees. She would have liked a round of applause, but the girls had been backing cars in the rain for seventy years and didn't get all excited about it. Then she flipped open her own phone. Text messages from Hayley, Alicia and Madison. Brit had forgotten the existence of Alicia and Madison. They seemed remote, dusty, people she might have known years ago.

Flo's phone rang. "Ninety seconds. I lose."

Four heads converged around the phone, but they waited for the message: "This is the Fitchburg Police Department. We're trying to locate Mrs. Aurelia Gibbs. She with you, Mrs. Heff? Her son is real concerned because she doesn't have her pills. You want to call us back? Then we can make sure everybody's fine and all. Thanks."

Brit forgot her own messages. She was too stunned by this one. He'd really done it.

At what point did a person call the police on his own mother? When he was so desperate for money he'd do anything? Or when he was genuinely worried about his mother's health?

The policeman sounded nice. They all sounded nice. Rose sounded nice. Sonya. Even Aston. Brit was deeply uneasy. She wished she could ask her parents about this. But it was too late now, and the slightest indication from her that something was wrong and their vacation would be ruined. In fact, no matter where Brit turned, somebody was going to be ruined.

"Bringing in the police is a master stroke," said Flo. "The police are now on Aston's side. If we need them, we can't call them."

"There they go!" cried Nannie. "And here we sit, camou-flaged. They'll never spot us."

"Where do we spend the night now?" said Aurelia. "I'm exhausted. And Flo's bruised."

"Let's stay in your farmhouse in Ashburnham," said Nannie.

Was it Brit's imagination or was Nannie increasingly not with the program? Aurelia had said over and over that her farmhouse was unheated and unlit.

"Aston emptied the farmhouse," Aurelia explained, as if she didn't remember saying it any more than Nannie remembered hearing it. "There are no beds, no food and no electricity. And how could I bear it, Nannie? I don't want to see my grandmother's dishes gone, my mother's apron and my father's woodworking tools gone, my little boy's first red wagon and sled gone. He was such a nice little boy, you know, that child of fifty years ago." Aurelia's chest was heaving. Her fingers clawed the air and strangled sounds came from her throat.

Without her medication, Aurelia was having a heart attack. Aston was right and it was Brit's fault. "Nannie! Shall I call 911?"

"She's just crying, Britsy."

They sat, uncomfortable witnesses to wrenching grief. Brit had cried like that over Coop.

"I thought I was a wonderful mother," whispered Aurelia. "I thought I gave Aston a wonderful childhood."

There was no comfort to offer. A college kid—Rupert, say—might still turn out okay after all. But after fifty-nine years, Aston was not going to turn out okay after all. All Brit could do was find a motel. There was a Super 8 near the Friendly's. In a million years Aston would never expect the girls to stay at a Super 8.

Brit drove over. If Aston really despised his mother, why would he care where she lived? Was he just plain mean or was even *more* money available if he kept her at Fox Hills? Rudely she asked, "Aurelia, what other money do you have?"

"My stock. He can't sell it without that power of attorney. I surmise he does have such a paper, having forged my signature. He hasn't let me see the monthly statements, so I don't know what my accounts are worth, and meanwhile the market has been fluctuating. Perhaps five million."

A man who didn't balk at selling his mother, her house and her wedding gown was not going to fade away when there was five million more.

Flo's right, she thought. We might need the police—and the police will be against us. We might need a doctor—and the doctor is against us. It's fun to call Coop but this isn't for fun. It's for real. We need that lawyer.

"Which reminds me," said Nannie, as if she too had five million dollars in stock, when nobody in Brit's family owned a single share of anything, "be sure not to tell your mother any of this, Britsy. Play your cards close to your chest."

Brit looked down. "My chest?" she said doubtfully.

"In bridge," explained Flo. "Or poker. When your cards are dealt, you don't hold them in the middle of the table for everybody to see and figure out how to beat you. You hold your cards close to your chest so nobody knows what you've got."

Brit promised to keep her cards close to her chest.

But she was not sure the girls were holding good cards.

She was not even sure they were playing with a full deck.

★ ★ ★

With everybody safely inside the Super 8, Brit had pizza delivered. She took pies to the girls and locked herself in her own room. Cross-legged in the middle of the bed, with her phone in one hand, a wedge of pizza in the other, the TV on mute, she read and listened to her messages. While Brit had been kidnapping old ladies, pocketing emerald bracelets and avoiding the police, Hayley had been dipping cones in chocolate sprinkles.

Tomorrow, Alicia and Madison would be having everybody over for pizza and wanted Brit to come and also spend the night. But tomorrow Brit had to take the girls to this lawyer and then drive them to Maine and, somewhere along the way, pick Daisy up.

It was impossible to explain any of this now, especially because Brit was so uneasy. She quick texted Hayley that they'd talk some other time and let Madison and Alicia know she couldn't come and left lengthy voice messages for Mom and Dad so they wouldn't be calling Nannie's house. She ate a bit of pizza and her phone rang.

She read the caller ID. *He likes me, he likes me!*

"I located the guy," Coop said briskly. "He's got his own Web site at the college where he used to teach, except he just retired."

She had forgotten that Coop was playing Internet detective.

"Aston's published one book, which I looked up on Amazon.com, and his sales rank is 1,527,998." Coop laughed. "When 1,527,997 people sell more books than you do, you don't have a bestseller."

The volunteer in the thrift shop had been more affectionate—the cop asking for Mrs. Heff—the store manager carrying luggage in the rain. "Is it still raining there?" she asked.

"Would I be here if it wasn't? I'm a prisoner in my own house. Good thing I had stuff to do online or I'd be crazy as well as bored."

She had cast Coop as her Woollie, walking her home from school, saying, I've always loved you.

"So that gives me a lot of leads to follow," said Coop. "Later." And he was gone.

121

He hadn't called to talk to her; he'd called to brag about his research skills. She already knew about those. Too well.

★ ★ ★

The girls were slow in the morning. It wasn't easy for them even to get up off the bed. They had to manage their medications. They had teeth to take care of (Nannie and Flo), or dentures (Aurelia). It was nearly nine before everybody had her face on and was ready to hit the road.

Nannie believed in being well dressed for reunions and for kidnapping a Buttermere. But this was the third day. Nannie could slide into her good old turquoise striped double knit pantsuit and the not-quite-matching navy blue turtleneck. Of course, she could have looked worse. There was a fire engine–print pantsuit from about 1975 that Brit really hoped was back home in a closet, dying.

"Britsy, I don't think we have to leave quite so early," said Nannie, who loved to be early. "Aurelia's appointment with the attorney isn't until eleven and it's just across the street, in that big office building next to the Sheraton."

"We have an errand to run first," said Brit. "Everybody in the car."

"What kind of errand could anybody have in Fitchburg?" said Flo skeptically.

"I made some phone calls last night," said Brit. "We have an errand in the village of Hubbardston."

"You run the errand," said Nannie. "We'll wait."

"Nannie, cut me some slack. I've schlepped you around. Now I need you to help me on this."

"Why?" demanded Flo.

"Because I asked you to."

Flo shrugged. "I need a better reason."

Brit had to bludgeon them into the Safari. They wouldn't stop demanding explanations, so she changed the subject and steered them into the past, where they were happier anyway. "Nannie, how come you married so late and had Mom so late?"

"I loved teaching Latin. I loved my little apartment. I married your grandfather when we were twenty-nine only because he couldn't stand it any longer. Back then, if it occurred to you to be intimate before marriage, you put it out of your mind. It was wrong and you might have a baby. So when your grandfather said, 'Marry me now or I have to find somebody else, because the wait is driving me crazy,' we got married. Then I had a miscarriage, a baby dead at birth, and another miscarriage before I had Gail."

Brit was aghast. "Mom never told me that."

"I never told her. Back then you didn't talk about such things. It was wrong to burden children with the problems of grown-ups."

Had Nannie held her dead baby? Had it been a boy or a girl? Had they named it? Did Nannie too visit a special grave, year in and year out?

"I could never have gotten through those sorrows without the girls," said Nannie.

If those babies had lived, I'd have aunts and uncles, thought Brit. Mom would be the youngest, instead of the only. I'd have cousins. We'd have the reunions.

She drove and drove. Hubbardston was nowhere. What were people thinking about when they said to each other, "I know! Let's live nowhere!"

But then the sun came out. First real sunshine in the entire month of June. Brit felt a million times better. She pulled up in front of a tiny white house with a red front door and honked. She put the stool and the ATW beside the car and nobody would get out, so she had to yell at them. Just as they were finally all lined up in the driveway, the red front door opened. A slender bride, her gown glistening with a thousand seed pearls, came slowly toward them, walking to music that couldn't be heard and holding the arm of a groom who couldn't be seen.

"It's my wedding gown," breathed Aurelia.

"Oh, Britsy," whispered Nannie. "How did you do it?"

"Brit telephoned me last night," said the bride, beaming. "The thrift shop people gave your wonderful granddaughter my number. I took the morning off from work, because what could be more important than this?"

Aurelia touched the beads with trembling fingers.

"It was a mistake for you to give away your gown," said the bride, "but it wasn't a mistake for me. May I give you my wedding photograph?"

It was a black-and-white portrait, and the couple looked old-fashioned and distant, as if they were really Aurelia and Woollie. "I'm hoping you'll let me keep your gown, Mrs. Gibbs, but if you need it, I'll wrap it in tissue for you."

"You keep it. It was worn in love. It was worn believing in Happily Ever After."

"And you did live Happily Ever After, didn't you?" said the bride.

Aurelia stroked the sleeve of the gown she had worn so long ago. "Yes," she lied, and Brit thought it was the nicest wedding present a person could give: the promise of Happily Ever After.

"So who is this attorney?" Brit asked Aurelia, who could not stop smiling at the wedding photograph.

"Woollie had an older brother who practiced law," she explained. "James died years ago. James's son Harrington took over the practice and then Harrington retired young. He's been playing golf in Georgia for—"

"She doesn't care!" yelled Flo. "Tell about Chloe Chandler."

"Florence, I've been hoping for sixty-five years your manners would improve."

"You hoped in vain," said Flo. "Tell about Chloe or I'll hit you over the head with a beach chair."

Brit laughed.

"Harrington's daughter Chloe took over the practice. She hardly knows Aston, because she's twenty-five years younger than he is."

How romantic to pick your lawyer from your long-lost husband's family. *This* lawyer could give Brit the second opinion she needed.

Brit went down the frontage road yet again, ignored the Sheraton and turned toward the office building. They were almost exactly on time for their appointment with Chloe Chandler, even though Hubbardston had been a longer drive than she had expected. But then, if you lived in the middle of nowhere, it stood to reason that getting back and forth would take a while.

"Choosing an attorney from sentiment is stupid," Flo told Aurelia. "You're asking for trouble."

"It pleases me," said Aurelia.

"Brit!" called Nannie. "There's a handicapped space! Park there."

"Are you feeling handicapped?"

"We do have a person with a walker," Flo reminded her.

I forgot that they're all eighty-six and half crippled, thought Brit. In the car, they're just girls.

Parked opposite the handicapped space was a beautiful gleaming black Porsche Carrera, the kind that could easily cost seventy-five or a hundred thousand dollars—she didn't keep up with prices of cars like this. Brit experienced serious car envy, her eyes lingering on every sleek detail of the Porsche.

Its license plate read ASTNIII.

CHAPTER 10

Back at Friendly's, the waitresses were just as friendly.

"It's my fault," said Aurelia drearily. "I saved every letter that came to me at Fox Hills. Everybody in our generation is a saver—string, pennies, envelopes. Remember how you used to write to me, Nannie? Every month from college graduation until Brit was born? I kept your letters in a lavender-scented box. I suppose they too were discarded when Aston disposed of my possessions."

"How come you stopped writing when I was born?" asked Brit.

"I was your babysitter. I was *seventy*. It was all I could do to feed and change you, never mind keep up my correspondence."

Brit had to think about that one: her birth had derailed Nannie's life.

"My bedside table at Fox Hills," said Aurelia, "was a metal canister with one shelf and one drawer. Life with one drawer—can you imagine?"

Flo got to the point. "So when Rose and Sonya took Aston through your room, they went through the drawer and found everything you kept there. Including letters."

"One letter in particular. I'm such an old fool. Chloe agreed to draw up my new will and stated the time, date and place of our meeting."

It could have been Aston below the Ashburnham cemetery. He would have guessed that his mother would visit Woollie's grave. Far above and through a haze of gravestones, perhaps even a Porsche was just another black roof. What rage he must have felt at Fox Hills, reading the letter that took away the money he thought he already owned. What a good actor he was, leaving Brit those pleasantly anxious little messages.

Outside Friendly's, the sky was turning purple, bruised by a coming storm.

"Let's just leave for Maine right now," said Flo. "Skip Chloe. After the reunion, we'll scare up another lawyer."

Aurelia shook her head. "Aston is impatient. He won't wait long. And because I am a timely person and am never late, when I do not appear at Chloe's office, he will assume you told the hotel clerk the truth, Flo. It's interesting that a man who always lies will think other people tell the truth. He will believe we have driven to Boston. Therefore I shall keep my appointment.

Woollie's grandniece will not let me down. It's been thirty minutes. Aston has assuredly given up. Brittany Anne, kindly drive us back to the office."

It took fifteen minutes to pay the bill, get everybody's nose powdered and load the girls back into the Safari. Yet again, Brit splashed down that frontage road. Aurelia was right. No Porsche was parked in front of the office. "I'll just make sure he isn't checking into or out of the hotel," Brit said, circling the Sheraton.

Wow, was it raining. It wasn't even rain. It was a deluge. Brit didn't want the girls out in this, wading through puddles, soaking their shoes and catching pneumonia. "How about if I go in first and make sure Chloe Chandler can still see you?" she suggested. "Because sometimes lawyers can't fit you in forty-five minutes later; they can only fit you in when you were expected. That way you don't get soaked unless we're sure."

"That is acceptable," said Aurelia.

Brit parked in the same slot she'd chosen to avoid police notice, half hidden by dripping leaves. Nobody commented on her desire to keep the van out of sight. In spite of Brit's brand-new jeans and a bright new T-shirt with a paint-fleck design, Nannie said, "Don't you have a nice little sundress to wear?"

Brit did not have a nice little sundress.

"At least carry my umbrella," said Nannie.

Brit did not carry things with a public television logo. She raced across the lots, skirting puddles. She had nothing with her except the phone in her jeans pocket. She was startled and pleased to find that she had automatically taken the car keys. It was like entry into a club—something related to driving was now procedure.

She tried to slide the keys into her empty jeans pocket, but her jeans fit well and the sharp bulge—there weren't just keys on the ring, but also a rental car ID—ruined her profile. She tucked the keys into her palm.

The law offices of Chandler & Chandler were on the first floor. The reception room had an English-country look, as if tea might soon be served on a tray. A coatrack held an immense black umbrella and a Burberry raincoat in the usual ugly dull plaid. Brit would never understand its popularity. How come even *two* people wanted it, never mind the world?

"It's still raining?" moaned the receptionist as Brit dripped all over the place. "I suppose it's cold out too?"

"Still cold," Brit agreed. "I'm here for Aurelia Gibbs. Is Chloe Chandler still free?"

The receptionist was puzzled. "You're here to pick Mrs. Gibbs up? But she never came."

"No, no, she sent me."

"Oh. Ms. Chandler will be delighted to see you." She dialed an extension. "A young lady is here on an errand from Aurelia Gibbs." The receptionist hung up, smiling at Brit. "Come this way."

This was perfect. Brit would have a chance to spill all her worries without the girls there.

Her jeans were drying from the heat of her skin. They were tight and clammy. Her hair was dripping. Once again she was a throg's neck. Pretending she looked great, she walked into the office, where a skinny blond woman really did look great in a black suit and a crimson scarf. The woman stood up to shake hands. "Chloe Chandler," she said harshly, as if announcing a wrestling competition.

Brit liked her severe clipped style. "Brit Bowman," she imitated. "I love your scarf," she added.

"Thank you. May I introduce Aston Gibbs?"

★ ★ ★

Brit had two choices.

She could bail. But the only place to run was the car. If she handed Aurelia over to Aston, Brit would fail the girls big-time.

This left choice number two. Bluffing.

So Brit beamed at Aston III and held out her hand. "I'm Nannie Scott's granddaughter! Brittany Bowman! I'm just along for the ride to the reunion. Gosh, I'm so glad to meet you, Mr. Gibbs. Everybody said you were like a total doll, and like they're so totally right." She pumped his hand vigorously.

Aston matched the furniture: gleaming and cultured. He looked scholarly and even handsome, in a wrinkled, balding way. He gave her a small, rather British smile, to match the Burberry raincoat that had to be his, and withdrew his hand. "The Reunion has such a pull on my mother. Are you thinking of attending college there? Have you arranged an interview with the admissions office?"

Rose had been absolutely right about his BBC accent. He could probably narrate a *Masterpiece Theatre* production and everybody would trust his credentials. Brit wasn't all that sure of her own acting ability, though, so she turned to Chloe. "Isn't it totally cool that all four roommates have gone to every single one of their reunions for sixty-five years? I hope I stay friends with *my* college roommates that long." Brit bounced a little, trying to look too young and stupid for college.

"Mrs. Bowman, you do not seem to realize the seriousness of this situation," said the lawyer.

"Now, Chloe," said Aston. "How could Ms. Bowman understand? She's receiving information from very confused sources. Ms. Bowman—may I call you Brittany?"

"Certainly," she said. Because only her friends called her Brit.

"I'm grateful that you are trying to help my unfortunate mother. I grasp the importance of the reunion to Aurelia, but this isn't a good idea. All the adult children of all four roommates kept their elderly mothers home last year, because home was best. It's best again this year. My mother is taking heavy-duty drugs to cope with her Alzheimer's, and without them, she'll deteriorate. No doubt being with her women friends has given her a surge of energy, but it won't last. I need to get my mother back to the excellent twenty-four-hour care at Fox Hills."

How was Brit going to get out of here without Aston tagging along and finding Aurelia? Where should she go with this bluff? She decided to switch from defense to offense. "My grandmother says Aurelia doesn't have Alzheimer's."

"I denied it at first too," agreed Aston. "It's a terrible diagnosis. Heartbreaking for sons and daughters." He sat back down. At his feet rested a large briefcase of butter-soft leather that Brit wanted to stroke.

Chloe gestured at Brit to have a seat too.

It would be like sitting down in the principal's office: Brit would be trapped. She crossed the room and perched on the windowsill. The window opened onto the back of the building, and a few feet away sat the Porsche. He had realized the car gave him away and moved it out of sight.

"Aurelia is sharp as a tack," Brit informed Aston and Chloe.

This was a Nannie-ism; people who were sharp as tacks had their marbles.

"Then she's having an excellent day," said Aston. "I'm glad. She has fewer and fewer of them. Alzheimer's is a strange disease. The mind and spirit can vanish for weeks, and then suddenly, one glimpses the old personality." He and Chloe looked at each other sadly. They weren't making it up. They were sad.

Now the very attorney Aurelia had chosen said gently—and nicely—"Long ago, Brittany, Aurelia Gibbs was married to my great-uncle. I've known her all my life. Every summer we used to get together at her farmhouse. I was also unwilling to believe the diagnosis of Alzheimer's. But since Aston called, I've spoken to Aurelia's doctor and to the staff. They said when she was admitted, she was in a state of complete paranoia, wildly accusing people of kidnapping her and screaming that she had been hijacked. She even accused her only son of stealing from her and forging her signature. Dr. White says it's common for the elderly to perceive that they are being badly used by their children, but for Alzheimer's patients, it's almost universal. Even so, Aurelia's behavior was extreme. She was ripping at people with her fingernails, kicking, trying to bite them! You need nursing staff to handle that kind of thing. Aston had no choice but to sign her in. And the people at Fox Hills have taken outstanding care of her."

Elegant well-mannered Aurelia—biting people? "But when she wrote to you," said Brit, "and asked for an appointment . . ."

"I have just found out that she did not write to me," said Chloe Chandler. "The letter I received was dictated by her college friend Florence Heff. Aurelia isn't mentally able to compose a letter anymore. Now, Ms. Bowman, nothing is going to happen to Mrs.

Heff. Mrs. Heff is not trying to wrongly influence or wrongly use her poor old friend. She thinks she's doing a good deed. But there cannot be a new will. Aurelia is *not* of sound mind."

Brit had not known that Flo had dictated the letter. Why hadn't Flo said so? Of the three girls, Flo was the most reliable, the most savvy. Nannie tended to drift. Aurelia saw what she wanted to see. But Flo . . .

Brit soldiered on. "Aurelia says Aston is just after her money and he's waiting for her to die and even bribing Dr. White with a marriage proposal so the doctor will change the medications and Aurelia will just get on with it and die quicker."

Chloe Chandler looked at Brit incredulously, and immediately Brit too was incredulous. How ridiculous this sounded. How melodramatic. Brit had fallen for every story the girls had given her. Aurelia, in her paranoia, had made things up; Nannie, in her need to believe that her dear roomies had lost no marbles, had passed on her own version; Flo had fallen for Aurelia's nonsense to the extent that she had picked up that cell phone of hers and dictated letters to Aurelia, thinking she was helping!

Just like my conversations with Coop, thought Brit. Any opening line he gives me, I fill in details with whatever makes me happy. I know perfectly well Coop is just bored and the minute the rain stops he'll be off on his bike trip and won't think of me again until calculus. But do I care about reality? No. I have us driving off in a Mini Cooper, which my parents are never going to buy me anyway, even though I can see it perfectly, sitting in my driveway. I'm no different from Aurelia. I'd rather live my dreams than my actual life.

She pressed her hands over her eyes.

"People with Alzheimer's," said Chloe, "are at a loss to explain the frightening world in which they find themselves. They thrash around in desperation because they can't understand what's going on, and they come up with conspiracy theories."

Aurelia *did* believe in a conspiracy. But of course a doctor wouldn't do any of those things. Any more than an attorney would lie.

"I remain hopeful that we're looking at medication problems," said Chloe. "Prescriptions are difficult to balance. Dr. White will adjust the levels as soon as Aurelia's back at Fox Hills. Then the awful sensation of having her plans circumvented will go away and Aurelia will feel much better."

Aurelia didn't want to feel better through drugs. She wanted to feel better by not being in Fox Hills. She wanted to feel better by going to the reunion.

"Brittany, help me get Aurelia the protection she needs," said Chloe.

Brit liked to believe that she was a lightning-fast thinker, but right now she was as slow as a 1980s computer. Pieces of thought dragged themselves meaninglessly through vacant brain space. "She thinks she needs protection from Mr. Gibbs."

"She does think that," agreed Chloe. "And in dealing with a paranoiac, we must admit that the terror is real for the patient. But that doesn't mean it's real."

Brit fell into the chair next to Aston after all. She'd known all along this was crazy. She stared at Aston's beautiful briefcase, unfastened, revealing neatly aligned folders, papers and a laptop edge.

"Actually," said Aston, "it's *Doctor* Gibbs." He was wearing a smirky little smile. "Perhaps we could work through your grandmother," suggested Aston. "Perhaps one of my mother's generation can coax her to be reasonable. I see you have your cell phone. Why don't you call your grandmother and she and I will discuss this?"

Brit took out her cell phone. She opened it. She clicked it on.

Aston leaned forward. "How rational is your grandmother?" he asked, frowning.

It was a need-to-know thing. Would any remaining rational old lady in the group raise her hand?

My grandmother, thought Brit, is totally rational, thank you. Furthermore, she thinks you are a goose end. I've trusted Nannie's judgment my whole life. If she says you're a goose end, Aston, you're a goose end.

Brit stood up. "Nannie doesn't use a cell phone. Different generation. I don't think we're going to be able to work this out after all. We won't reschedule the meeting, Ms. Chandler. But thank you for your time."

Aston too stood, as a gentleman does when a lady is departing.

He grabbed her wrist, clenched it hard, forced her fingers open and took her car keys.

CHAPTER 11

Without car keys, Brit could do nothing. She couldn't save the girls or take them to the reunion. She was helpless.

So this was how Aurelia felt. And how Nannie felt when Mom chopped up her driver's license.

Chloe stepped between Brit and Aston, a good thing, because Brit was seriously eager to follow Aurelia's example and use her nails and teeth. In her wrestler voice, Chloe snapped at Brit, "Just who do you think you are? How dare you decide whether Dr. Gibbs can see his mother? How dare you decide whether Aurelia Gibbs sees her attorney? Your behavior is reprehensible. You take Dr. Gibbs to his mother right now."

Brit wanted to kick her in the shins and swear at her. "You're supposed to be representing Aurelia!" Brit yelled. "But instead you're representing her son. Flo told Aurelia it was stupid to pick a lawyer because of some old family emotion. And Flo was right. You're unethical! You're uncompetent!"

"*In*competent," Aston corrected her.

She hated him. She hated Chloe. "If you're so close to Aurelia, Chloe, how come you didn't know her mind had gone? How come you agreed to rewrite her will to start with?" she demanded.

Chloe arranged papers on her desk.

"If you're so close to your great-aunt, how come yesterday was the first time you ever talked to her doctor?" yelled Brit.

Chloe rearranged the papers on her desk.

"How often did you visit Aurelia?" Brit bet the answer was never. Her cell phone rang. Both Aston and Chloe brightened, as if planning to snatch that out of her hands too.

A phone call was the last thing she needed. It wasn't Mom's ring, thank God. Brit checked her caller ID: Florence Heff—the one girl who might really know what Brit should do next. "Aston is right here in the law office," she yelled to Flo. "Chloe Chandler is *his* attorney, not Aurelia's. They aren't going to let me go until I tell them where you guys are staying." She was proud of that—implying that the girls were gathered in a room somewhere instead of a car a few hundred yards away.

"Nonsense," said Flo. "Shoulder them out of your way."

"Aston took my car keys," yelled Brit, "so I can't drive back to your place."

"Let me talk to Aston," said Flo grimly. "Right now!"

Brit was relieved. She handed over the phone. Now Aston

would catch it. Flo knew how to do anything. "Aston," bellowed Flo, and not only Chloe and Brit but probably the secretary down the hall heard Flo just fine, "This is Florence Heff. Your mother is eighty-six years old. What difference does it make to you whether she takes a particular medication or sleeps in a particular bed?"

"I love her," said Aston in the tone of voice of a son whose love is really stretched. In fact, in the exact tone of Brit's father when he felt like throwing her into the middle of next week.

Every time Brit thought she knew what was what, she didn't.

Who had all their marbles?

Who were the good guys?

Who were the bad guys?

"You stop this nonsense, Aston Gibbs!" shouted Flo. "You haven't cared about anything except her money in thirty years. Well, you're not getting it. She's changing her will and since she can't go to this lawyer, she'll go to another one. You lose, Aston. No more money pouring out of this particular faucet. Furthermore, she's going to do a full audit of everything you've sold illegally and retrieve every cent you've stolen from her."

Aston, sighing, handed Brit's phone to Chloe.

"Attorney Chandler here," said Chloe harshly. "We're moving into difficult territory, Mrs. Heff. You have been turning an ill and confused woman against her own son and against her own doctor. However, I think the problems can be resolved in a meeting. I recognize that you are uncertain about the motives of Dr. Gibbs, but I, being a lawyer, have only the motive of justice and, as one with a personal and long-term relationship to Aurelia, will take great care to do what is best for her circumstances."

Brit's father hated lawyers. He had a whole stock of lawyer jokes he was always e-mailing to people. It did not surprise Brit when Flo yelled, "Yeah, right! Like you're pure!"

Chloe moved into kindergarten-teacher mode. "Now you just calm down, Mrs. Heff, and let me take charge," she said, now speaking to a five-year-old. *You obey me,* she was saying, just as Brit had said on the ferry. *I will take away your privileges if you don't. You are no longer a grown-up.*

"Oh, all right," said Flo, giving in. "Put Brit back on the line."

Brit was stunned. Flo? Florence Mirsky-whoever-the-first-two-husbands-were-Heff? Yielding in one minute?

Brit snatched the phone. She wanted to Lysol it now that Aston's and Chloe's fingerprints were all over it. Out of the phone came a whisper as thick and windy as a vacuum cleaner: *"Keep them busy. I'm calling a taxi and getting us out of here. We'll meet later."*

It was all Brit could do not to giggle. Flo would hustle the girls into a taxi and scurry off to parts unknown—heads down, identity hidden. Flo was going to have a great time.

Brit had to bluff much better this time than she had before. Flo hung up, but Brit continued to talk as if settling details. "Okay," she said at intervals. "Well . . . um . . . okay, but . . . Okay, sure, Flo. Right. I'll tell them."

How fast were taxis in Fitchburg?

Did they even *have* taxis in Fitchburg?

How long would she have to play games for the girls to get away? It could take five minutes just to transfer the girls from Safari to taxi. And who would do the transferring? Flo couldn't toss her own step stool down. Did taxi drivers do that for you?

140

And where would Flo take the girls? How would Brit find them again?

She had to blush over that one. She—like Nannie—had forgotten about cell phones.

"They're taking turns in the bathroom," she told Chloe. "They have to powder their noses. They all have digestive problems. They're always on bathroom emergency status. Nannie, for example—"

"I don't think we need details," said Chloe.

Brit held the silent phone to her ear. She studied her fingernails. She was sick of her current color and design. And then, to her horror, the phone rang. Oh, no! She had automatically turned it off. "Honestly! Flo accidentally disconnected me! Now she's calling back," she said. Like they'd believe that. But she kept bluffing. "Hi, Flo," she said to Cooper James.

"It's Coop," he said, proving he was not the swiftest thinker in the conspiracy.

"I said, *Hi, Flo!*" she bellowed.

Not surprisingly, there was silence at Cooper's end.

"Okay!" she yelled. "Try not to worry too much! Maybe it'll work out for the best."

"It's Coop," repeated Cooper. "I have really important things to tell you. First of all, when Aston—"

"Later!" shouted Brit, turning the phone off. She killed a few more precious seconds fitting the phone into her jeans pocket and smoothing the denim over the bulge. At last she looked at Chloe. "I don't exactly know how you think I'm going to take Aston to Aurelia. *He* has my car keys," she pointed out.

"And I'm keeping them," said Aston. "I don't want you driving off into the wild blue yonder. I'll drive us both in my car."

Brit had sat through as many safety assemblies in school as every other kid in America. She never paid any attention. But clear as another phone ringing, she heard a police officer on the stage at high school saying, Never never never get in a car with somebody who is threatening you.

"Good plan," said Chloe to Aston. "I have another appointment, so I can't go along, but keep me posted."

"What about my keys?" Brit said to Aston.

"When I'm reunited with my mother, I will return your keys."

If caving in was good enough for Flo, it was good enough for Brit, so she caved in to Aston and walked in defeat back to the waiting room. Aston paused for his raincoat, and Brit paused with him. While he was managing sleeves and buttoning himself up and closing his briefcase over his reams of paper and smoothing what was left of his hair, Brit snatched her car keys out of his hand and bolted. She was out the door and into the parking lot before he could react. She bet that Aston would not want to get his feet, hair, suit or even thoughts wet, and that would give her enough time to get into her car and lock the doors after her. She prayed the girls were safely gone.

The little trees on every parking island were drooping with rain. Even the high shiny Safari was difficult to spot. She hesitated, wasting crucial seconds, saw the van, raced up, ripped open the driver door, flung herself in and locked it.

Aurelia and Flo were gone, but Nannie was not. She was sitting up front in the passenger seat. She handed Brit a beach towel, presumably from the summer suitcase. "Dry your hair, dear. I don't want you to catch your death of cold."

"But Nannie—"

"Flo and Aurelia took the taxi to Friendly's, the driver was such a dear man, so helpful, but I couldn't leave you here by yourself, Britsy. Aston is the sort of person who would do anything, you know."

"You're here to protect *me*?" said Brit. It was ludicrous. Nannie was not protection; Nannie was liability. Brit shoved the key into the ignition. Her soaked jeans had tightened up so much the cell phone was poking her thigh. She stretched out, loosened the pocket, got her phone and stuck it in a cup holder. There was something else down in her pocket, but she didn't have time to extricate that as well, so she threw the van into reverse.

"Wear this," said Nannie, "so Aston won't recognize you as we depart." She lifted bright orange hair toward Brit.

Flo had been wearing a wig. The whole concept of wigs was appalling, unless it was Halloween. Brit was not wearing somebody else's used, still-warm orange wig. And what did Flo's head look like now? Was it bald and speckled and shiny? Beautifully dressed Flo? "Nannie," Brit began.

Brit had been right that Aston wouldn't want to get wet and wrong that it would slow him down. He had driven after her in his Porsche. Now he pulled up behind the Safari, so that his car was at a right angle to her rear bumper. She was trapped: curb and tree in front, Porsche behind.

I could give it a little gas and slam backward through his Porsche, like a demolition derby driver, she thought.

But since her personal goal was to retain her driver's license, crushing cars was out. She put the van in park. The thing in her pocket continued to bother her. It's the diamond and emerald bracelet, she thought. She had transferred it from one pair of pants to the other, meaning to give it back to Aurelia.

Aston got out of his car and walked over to the Safari. "Where is my mother?" he shouted through her closed window.

Brit didn't know how long Aston was prepared to stand in the rain, but she personally had half a pound cake, some peanut brittle, all the macaroons and several bottles of water.

"Roll your window down half an inch, Britsy, so we can talk," said her grandmother. "Otherwise, the situation might continue indefinitely."

Nannie's demeanor could go back and forth so quickly between dithery old lady and stern Latin teacher. Brit lowered her window half an inch.

Mist covered Aston's face and settled in his hair. He gave Brit an embarrassed look.

His voice, covered by the rhythmic spatter of rain on the car roof, was too low for Nannie to hear.

"I apologize. I was trying to protect my mother and I handled it poorly. I need to give you a single fact about this situation, Brittany. I don't want your grandmother to hear because it would only upset her. But you cannot fully grasp what's going on unless you have the whole truth. Please hear me out. Once you know the whole situation, you'll be able to do the right thing."

Aston walked back to his Porsche and opened the passenger door. Brit was a little surprised it could be opened, because in her side mirror it looked as if he was too close to the Safari. If she did smash her way out, she'd crush only the trunk of the Porsche. Flo would approve.

Aston was just getting his umbrella. He came back and stood patiently under its shelter. Umbrellas were so boring and middle class. Your really vicious creep didn't care if he got wet. Your college professor, worn out by his loony mother, still cared. And

144

Aston still cared, because the wetness on his face was not rain. It was tears. He took from an inner pocket a pressed handkerchief, and in exactly the same way his mother had patted away her tears over him, he patted away *his* tears over *her*. Then he folded the hanky carefully and put it in his pocket with equal care.

That's how he's tried to treat his mother, thought Brit. With care. His method is lousy, his timing is lousy, but Mom and Dad were right all along. He's doing the best he can.

"Brittany," said Aston, "lock your grandmother in the van, if it makes you feel better, and leave the keys with her. I truly regret being childish in the law office. My mother has backed me into a corner. You need to understand what that corner is."

Aston had left the passenger door of his Porsche open. If another downpour began—and it would—his upholstery would be ruined. He really and truly was putting his mother's welfare ahead of his possessions, because a Porsche was some possession.

"Be right back, Nannie," she told her grandmother. She got out of the Safari, flicking the control so all the doors would lock when she slammed hers, and joined Aston, who had backed up a few yards. He generously shifted his umbrella so that she too was under it.

He smiled sadly at her. There was nothing smirky in it. I'm a horrible person, thought Brit. I'm exactly like Coop. It's a rainy day and I'm using Aurelia and Aston's catastrophe to entertain myself.

Brit should have followed her instincts and gone straight home back when Nannie fell on the ferry stairs.

"You, Ms. Bowman," said Aston III, "are in an unfortunate position."

His face was changing. His jaw was tightening, his eyes were glittering and a little muscle in his cheek was jumping. "As is clear from the pendant on your key chain," he said, spitting out his consonants, "this van is a rental car, which you are too young to drive. A minor crime, but it indicates that you do not care about the law. You have stolen a helpless confused old woman from the safety of her hospital bed, even though you knew that her doctors and her son would refuse to let you take her. At the same time, you stole her jewelry. A witness saw you pocket a bracelet. During the night, you worked on the simple mind of a defenseless old lady who quite literally doesn't have enough sense to get out of the rain. You, Ms. Bowman, knowingly deprived Aurelia Gibbs of medications necessary to her health. You," he said in a tight thin whisper, "are a sadist who preys upon the elderly."

The gray of the sky and the black of the pavement moved toward each other, suffocating her in between them.

"I can prove it in court," he said. A weird glad smile decorated his face. "I have a doctor, two aides and an attorney who will testify to it. How will you explain yourself to the police, Ms. Brittany Anne? How will you explain yourself to a judge? I'm going to call the television stations myself, so you won't have a chance to clean up first. I want the world to see the drowned rat who is whisking these elderly husks from one motel to another, manipulating them, depriving them of food, not permitting them to rest, fooling with their medication." Aston flicked his umbrella. Water lashed Brit's face. "And most shocking of all, instead of letting my mother go to her attorney when my mother was desperate for help, *you* went. *You* are deciding whether or not an eighty-six-year-old woman should have an attorney."

"It isn't like that," she whispered.

He laughed. "Look at you. A dirty teenager in filthy sneakers and a disgusting T-shirt. You think your word will stand up against mine? You look as if you commit arson for pay. Your grandmother, an old bat who can't even comb her hair, will have to try to find you a lawyer and get you bail. Since that is beyond her capacity, she'll have to call your parents, who will then be accused of letting you run wild. They'll probably lose custody of you."

The rain pounded down on Brit. She stared at feverish red spots in Aston's cheeks. Not only could he destroy her, he wanted to. And he would destroy her parents along with her.

If she accused Aston of a string of lies, who would listen? Who would pay attention when Nannie insisted that the professor, the doctor and the lawyer were all goose ends? What would a judge think when Flo said, Oh, just run over his feet.

How easily she had fallen for his act yet again. She had been safe in a locked car in a public place and *willingly got out*! How could she fault the doctor or the lawyer when they fell for his acting too?

He had wrecked his mother's life with these lies. He probably had fun, writing his own script, reading his own play, acting his own roles. Spending somebody else's money.

"You know what else, Brittany Anne?" he said. "It won't be my mother who dies first. It will be your grandmother. When you're arrested, she'll have a heart attack. Her death will be your responsibility."

Nannie would die? And it would be Brit's fault?

"Yoo-hoo, Britsy!" Nannie's voice warbled out into the rain.

"Or," said Aston, "telephone my mother. Explain what I will

147

do to you, and she will agree to sign over everything. And then—how nice, Brittany Anne—you have a future after all."

"Yoo-hoo!" Nannie had gotten out of the Safari. Armed with her PBS umbrella, she was preparing to swing it like a baseball bat to save Brit. On her arm hung her purse, the immense bag without which she never stirred. How thin was the forearm supporting that weight, how trembly the hands gripping that umbrella. She was a full foot shorter than Aston, her white hair flattened and her turquoise double knit spattered by the rain. Her battle cry was "Yoo-hoo!"

Brit had never loved her so much.

But their enemy simply collected the PBS umbrella and held it too high for Nannie or Brit to reach. Now he held two big umbrellas over two little women, and any observer would have thought him such a gentleman when what he was really holding over Brit was a threat. "Phone call?" he reminded her.

Brit *could* say scornfully, We're going to the reunion, you scumbag.

She *could* get back in the Safari, put it in reverse, slam the gas pedal to the floor and rip the rear right fender off his precious Porsche.

She *could* yell, I'm finding Aurelia a new home! So there!

But he was not bluffing. He had probably parked that Porsche behind her *because* a crushed car would be proof of the uncontrollable and vicious temper of the accused sixteen-year-old girl.

I can't give in to him, she thought. I have to keep protecting Aurelia.

But every daydream Brit had ever had would be destroyed once Aston went ahead. Every daydream would be replaced by a nightmare. He might want to destroy Brit even *more* than he wanted the rest of Aurelia's money. Destroying Brit would be such fun, such a challenge, so many lies.

She saw her life rained out, running into a storm drain. She saw her mother's stunned face when she had to deal publicly with such horrible accusations; she saw her father's disbelief—his darling daughter? She saw the media, cameras zooming in on her parents, exposing them to the entire nation: people who had so badly reared their child that the child had grown up to prey upon helpless old women.

She patted her pocket for her cell, but she'd tossed it into the cup holder. She took a few steps back to the Safari and opened the driver door, the doors all having unlocked when Nannie opened her door.

Nannie was puzzled.

Aston was smirking.

Brit reached way over the front seat but the cup holder was too far. She had to get on the running board and lean over the seat. She didn't see the orange wig. She must have hurled it into the back. The image of Flo sacrificing her elegance for Aurelia's sake and ripping off that wig made Brit weep. All the girls were braver than she was. Flo would endure public humiliation. Nannie would attack a man twice her size.

And Brit? Brittany Anne Bowman was apparently not willing to suffer even a tiny little bit for another person's sake.

It came to her that although some things were so yesterday, more things were always today.

Trust.

Friendship.

The girls had given her second chances all through this trip;

they had let her be part of the team after all; they trusted her. Whatever the cost, Brit had to stand up for Aurelia.

She turned to inform Aston that she was not giving up after all, but Aston had shoved Nannie into the front passenger seat of his Porsche and was slamming the door. He raced around his car, leaped into the driver's seat and started the engine.

Brit ran forward and clawed at Nannie's locked door, but the Porsche—which could go from zero to sixty in six seconds— did so.

Aston Gibbs drove away with Nannie.

CHAPTER 12

Brit had one advantage: she didn't care what happened to a rental car.

Aston took off like a shot but immediately slowed down in a careful expensive-car-owner kind of way. Even so, in the time it took Brit to start her engine, fasten her seat belt, look for traffic and pedestrians, back up and go after him, he was out of sight.

When she tore through a puddle he had avoided, the van hydroplaned. It was scary, but it didn't slow her down. In fact, she drove faster, as if she could cut down on the effect of water on tires by adding speed. No wonder insurance companies charged more for teenagers, she thought, taking more risks. She bounced over the railroad tracks and went around the bend of the frontage road just in time to see Aston turn right on Route 12. By the time she arrived at the light, it was red again. Stopping for red lights was so yesterday. Brit ran the light, whipped into traffic and forced oncoming cars to brake or hit her. Luckily, they braked.

Aston could turn off this main road anywhere and hide on some little side street, chuckling as she flew past. She had to assume that he wasn't doing that, that she could catch up.

Her mind flew as fast as the car.

Taking Nannie was not rational. He could not actually *want* an eighty-six-year-old. There could be only two reasons for him to grab Nannie. The logical reason was leverage: this would certainly make Aurelia give him everything. The illogical reason was taking an old woman for the fun of it.

If it was the first reason, Aston wouldn't want Nannie injured or dying. He wanted to exchange her. So Brit needed to call Aurelia right now, to make Aurelia call Aston and promise him anything.

But if it was the second reason . . . and it might be; if he had been the black car at the foot of the cemetery hill, he didn't want to resolve the situation; he wanted to prolong it and entertain himself in some sick way. And meanwhile, what might Aston Gibbs do to Nannie?

Her grandmother—in the hands of a man who would do anything.

It struck Brit how little she actually listened to anybody. Over and over, the girls had said Aston would do anything.

If Aston turned right off Route 12, he'd enter downtown Fitchburg, where the thrift shop was. If he kept going, they'd come to that rotary, with all its choices. She placed her bets on the rotary. The next two lights were against her but she weaseled through anyway. And there he was, barely visible. The black finish on the Porsche winked at her.

"You hurt my grandmother," she screamed toward his car, "and I'll kill you!"

She felt all too capable of it. Her fingers tightened around the wheel as if it were a murder weapon. She flipped her phone open and drove one-handed—in the rain, in traffic, going fast—and knew how people had fatal accidents. But the only fate she cared about now was Nannie's.

Cars turned off. There were just two vehicles between them now: a white SUV and a red mason's dump truck. Their bulk prevented Brit from seeing where Aston went next.

She pressed her way through the numbers stored on her phone.

At the rotary, cars meshed like links on a chain. The SUV and the dump truck came to a full stop. There was no room to pass them on the left or on the right, legally or illegally.

"Brit?" said Flo.

Brit entered the rotary. Aston was gone. He could have taken any direction. She went the way she had before for no reason except she knew the road. "Aston grabbed Nannie," she summarized for Flo. "Kidnapped her like he kidnapped Aurelia. Shoved her in his car and took off. You told me he would do anything, but I didn't believe you. I was right behind him in the Safari, but I've lost him."

Flo gasped. "Aurelia and I are at Friendly's. Same old booth. You drive back and we'll come up with a plan."

Did she think Brit was going to sit around at Friendly's and order pancakes? "I'm not turning back. He could hurt Nannie. Make Aurelia phone Aston and promise him anything."

"He won't hurt Nannie," said Flo. "He sees himself as a pillar of society, an important man admired by his academic colleagues. There's no point in driving madly after somebody you've lost. Turn around."

"I'm not turning around. It would be abandoning Nannie." She couldn't slow down either, even when she was speeding to nowhere. She hoped those little kids on bikes knew better than to play in the road today.

"I'm on the phone with you now, Brittany Anne," said Aurelia. "I will phone my son immediately and submit to all his demands. He won't hurt Nannie. I'm sure he's already horrified at what he did and wondering how to get out of it. The moment I promise him all that he wants, he'll bring her back, and we'll all pretend nothing happened."

"*I'm* not going to pretend nothing happened!"

"Where are you now?" asked Aurelia.

"West on Twelve."

"He might be headed for the farmhouse. After all, hostages are difficult to take into motels and restaurants. I'll give you instructions for a shortcut. Aston won't take it. Potholes. He doesn't risk his cars on that kind of surface. While you're driving there, I'll call him."

Brit flung the Safari down the road Aurelia described. Woods closed in. The shortcut was one of those roads where you could break down and nobody would ever find you. This made her think of calling the police. But Aston would pull out the senility card and the paranoia card and the depraved-teenage-girl card, and the police would believe him, not Brit.

Her phone rang. "What did Aston say?" she yelled into it. "Is Nannie okay?"

"It's me, Coop."

"Get off my phone!" she screamed at him.

"Brit! Don't hang up on me! I have to tell you what Aston—"

There was no time for stupid interruptions. She disconnected, hit Flo's number and got through. How come Flo's phone wasn't busy, with Aurelia and Aston discussing details? "What did Aston say?" she shouted.

"He's not answering," said Aurelia. "I left a message."

Not answering?

"He's doing it to scare us," said Aurelia. "There's nothing we can do now but wait."

Tears coursed down Brit's face. The tears were extremely hot, as if she had reached a boiling point.

Oh, Nannie! Last week, you were joyful in your kitchen, full of secret plans for rental car deliveries. You were dreaming of charging the evil castle of Fox Hills and rescuing the princess Aurelia. You were wearing your old bibbed apron with the big pockets, opening your sixty-year-old cookbook to the same old page, baking your famous chocolate pound cake, tucking it in Tupperware and carefully writing the label. And now . . .

She drove on and on. Who would want to live in these deep gloomy woods, without neighbors?

I have to call the police. Nannie's safety comes first. If I dial 911, who will I get? I'm not in Fitchburg now. What do I tell them? I don't know where *I* am, let alone where *Aston* is. I'll sound like a crazy person.

I *am* a crazy person.

And there were the sagging old farmhouse and the rusty

155

pump. Since yesterday, tires had compressed the tall grass. Brit turned the Safari and drove over the tracks. Branches whapped her windshield, and twigs snapped under her wheels.

Then she was off the grass and on dirt where once tractors and wagons had stood, and cows and horses had walked, and now a Porsche was parked. Aston was standing in the rain, opening the passenger door. Brit could see Nannie's white hair.

Two could play the block-your-car game. Brit jerked the wheel, planning to pull parallel to the driver's side of the Porsche so Aston couldn't leave. Who knew that mud was as slippery as ice? The Safari skidded when she braked, engulfing the Porsche in a spray of black mud. Braking again had no effect. The Safari just kept going until it reached a dry patch.

Aston was screaming, but Brit was screaming more. She ripped out the keys almost before the Safari stopped moving, leaped out, charged through the mud and got to Nannie's side all in the time it took Aston to shake his fist once.

The words that poured out of Brit's mouth were an assortment she had not often used. They were certainly not words Nannie ever used. "If you've hurt my grandmother, Aston Gibbs, I'll kill you!" she finished.

"She isn't hurt! Look what you did to my car!"

"I didn't do anything to your car. That's mud! If I do something to your car, you'll know it! I'll key it, I'll smash it, I'll throw rocks at it! Nannie, are you all right?"

Nannie was trembling and clinging to her huge purse. "Britsy," she wailed. She was tangled in the chest strap of her seat belt, her right arm snagged and sticking out sideways. Brit tried to guide Nannie's arm free but her grandmother wouldn't let go of her purse.

"It's okay, Nannie," she said, trying to lower her voice to comfort level. She couldn't do it. She was still screaming. "Everything's okay now."

"It's not okay," said Nannie, starting to cry. "He punctured me. Like Eeyore. Remember the balloons at his birthday?"

Aston had sent Nannie over the edge. Nannie had lost her marbles.

Brit lifted her fist at Aston, sharp keys sticking out between her knuckles. "I'll put your eyes out!" she shrieked. "How dare you touch my grandmother! You call your mother right now. You negotiate with her. You can't negotiate with me because I'll kill you!"

She knew she looked like a soaking-wet madwoman.

Because I *am* a soaking-wet madwoman, she thought.

"She isn't punctured," said Aston irritably. "She's just senile."

"Don't you dare use that word about my grandmother! You have ten seconds to get Aurelia on the phone or I get the Ashburnham police. You can try to ruin my life, Aston Gibbs, but I will drag you down with me."

Nannie's purse had turned upside down and its contents had fallen onto her lap or tumbled to the floor of the Porsche. "Britsy, my Chap Stick!" cried Nannie. "My Bic pen!"

"I'll get you new ones," said Brit, feeling that her edges were coming unsewn; she was a pillow whose stuffing was oozing out. She unwound the seat belt, freed Nannie's arm and helped Nannie swing her feet around. The Porsche was low. It was harder to get out of a low vehicle than a high one. "You put your hands on my shoulders, Nannie, and I'll put my hands on your waist, and up you'll come."

Nannie stood up. A crochet hook and assorted credit cards tumbled from her lap into the mud.

Into his cell phone, Aston said, "Hello, Mother."

"My things, Britsy!" cried Nannie, stretching toward half a paperback. Nannie had the maddening habit of ripping pages off after she read them. Fractions of book littered her house from when she had gotten bored with a mystery novel at page fifty and abandoned the remains. Brit handed Nannie her paperback shreds and then Nannie worried about the envelope that held her grocery coupons.

Brit wasn't sane, never mind patient. She had to get Nannie out of there and get them home. Forget that part about how home is where the heart is. Home is where the lock is. Where the door shuts tightly and the bad guys are on the other side.

"That's not enough, Mother," said Aston. "I want the papers dated last year."

Why, you scum, thought Brit. You *did* forge everything. And if Aurelia does what you're asking, and she backdates the power of attorney you faked, it'll be *unforged*. You'll have *unstolen* the money.

"Britsy!" wailed Nannie, trying to reach her cataract sunglasses. "Take my purse."

The purse was so heavy Brit didn't know why Nannie's arm hadn't snapped off. No wonder her shoulders were rounded. Brit opened the bag so she could stuff Nannie's junk back in, and Flo's orange hair stared back up at her. I'll be the one to die of a heart attack, thought Brit. Instead, she wept for her grandmother's marbles.

"That will be sufficient, Mother," said Aston. "However, you *are* returning to Fox Hills. You are not well." His voice got smirky. "You cannot be allowed to wander around."

Wander around and tell people the truth about you, thought Brit grimly. She hoisted the ten-ton purse, took Nannie's arm and walked her over the mud to the van. The step stool sank into the soft dirt and then Nannie was too tired even to step high enough to get on the stool and Brit was just a desperate kid with a shivering old woman. By the time she finally got Nannie into the front seat, they were both sobbing. Brit got mud all over her face when she brushed away the tears so she could see well enough to drive.

The desire to kill Aston had passed. The only desire she had now was to drive away, drive anywhere, just not be there.

She slammed the doors, locked the two of them in and turned in a wide circle, keeping as far as possible from the worst of the mud. When all four tires were safely on grass and she had traction again and they weren't going to get stuck in this awful place, she looked back at Aston Gibbs.

He was leaning against the peeling white siding of the old farmhouse and he was laughing.

He'd had a great afternoon. He got to threaten a kid, fake out a lawyer, shove an old lady around, accelerate from zero to sixty in six seconds, taunt his mother . . . and get rich.

As soon as she was out of sight—maybe before—he would be jumping up and down on the old porch. *I'm rich, I'm rich! I won, I won!* he would shout.

And then he would go on laughing for years to come.

Laughing at Brit, who had lost; at Nannie, who had lost her marbles; and at Aurelia, who had lost all hope and freedom.

CHAPTER 13

Nannie slept on Flo's pillows while Brit endlessly checked the traffic behind her for a black Porsche.

I lost my chance to call the police, she thought. If I'd called 911 when I was driving down Williams Road, Aston would have been caught in the act of kidnapping. He could maybe have explained if he had his own mother in the Porsche, but he sure couldn't have explained why he had Nannie. But I didn't call. There's nobody to take my side or Aurelia's against Aston now.

If only she had remembered to use the camera on her phone ... She could have gotten a picture of Aston standing there in the rain.

Except even then, he could probably have figured out a lie to explain it.

She was back at the rotary without any recollection of the return trip.

The phone rang. It was Cooper James.

She could only vaguely recall being interested in Coop. "Hi," she said. She hardly had enough energy to form syllables. "I can't talk now, Coop."

"Then just listen. Don't hang up on me. What I found out in newspaper archives was that Aston had a lot of trouble in his marriages. In two of them, the wife got a restraining order against him, which he didn't obey, and he went after her and ended up in jail with assault charges. The guy is dangerous, Brit."

Nannie had been alone in the car with a guy twice jailed for assault charges?

If she had called the police, they'd have checked Aston's record and they'd have been on Brit's side after all. But she couldn't even prove he'd ever taken Nannie, and Nannie had lost her marbles.

What if she had gone to Friendly's and sat patiently with Flo and Aurelia in a booth? What would Aston have done? Forced Nannie down cellar stairs, past empty shelves where once applesauce had sat in jars, into the dark with a dirt floor and spider-covered walls? What would have happened next?

Brit was suddenly out of everything. Out of strength. Out of plans. Out of hope.

She turned the phone off and kept driving, desperate to see Friendly's and turn Nannie over to Flo and Aurelia.

★ ★ ★

Chloe had arranged for a private conference room in the Sheraton for the following morning, so Brit and the girls got rooms in the Sheraton for that night and even had dinner in the public dining room, as if things were normal.

"I can't believe Chloe went along with everything," said Brit. "A minute ago you were supposedly too gaga to sign anything, but now you're just fine and you can sign away your life?" She couldn't stand to think of Aston smirking in Chloe's office at that moment. While Chloe fine-tuned the paperwork that would make Aurelia nobody and Aston somebody. "I thought you'd keep fighting now that Nannie's safe," Brit said to Aurelia. "I thought Buttermeres never surrendered. But no—he *wins* everything and you *lose* everything." Brit was ashamed of herself for harping on this. Who was Brit to talk about not surrendering? But she wanted Aston to *pay*. She wanted it to be *fair*. The bad guy shouldn't win.

"The arrangement isn't entirely bad. Aston wins the money he wants," said Aurelia, "but I win the freedom I want."

"What freedom?"

"Aurelia's going to live with me," said Flo. She had covered her head with a green cotton scarf and looked like a lightbulb or a cancer patient. Brit reminded herself to dig out the wig, the last thing on earth she felt like touching, except for Aston.

"I own the largest condo in my retirement center. Aurelia will have a much larger bedroom than she had at Fox Hills and an excellent bathroom with marble counters. Not a step or a stair in the place and lots of activities for old skunks like us. Nannie, darling, you've hardly touched your soup. Would you rather have scrambled eggs and toast? Eggs can be so soothing. Are you all right, Nannie?"

Nannie had to ask Brit's opinion. "Am I all right, Britsy?" she said anxiously.

I can't go on, thought Brit. I can't put that step stool down one more time for one more eighty-six-year-old to climb on. We haven't even gotten Daisy. We have speeches and chicken dinners to go. And that pile of beach chairs—I just know I'll be carrying them down some rocky cliff plus making sure the girls and their beach bags don't fall off, and then I'll have to get everybody back up.

She took a deep breath. "I think you're all right, Nannie. In fact, I think you may be the world's oldest living kidnap victim as well as the oldest living kidnapper."

Nannie didn't smile. Aurelia didn't smile. Not even Flo smiled.

But how could Aurelia ever smile again? Aurelia had to live with the fact that her son—her only child—had turned out greedy, mean and dangerous, and Aurelia could never look back at any of her life without being assaulted by that.

"How about a nice hot bath, Nannie?" said Brit. "It'll be so relaxing. Let's go up to your room. I'll help you in and out of the tub."

They all tottered out of the dining room, even Brit. They sagged in the elevator and barely made it to their rooms. Brit ran a tub for Nannie. She helped Nannie take off her shoes and undo her buttons and then went into the bathroom to check how hot the water was. When she came back out, Nannie was sitting on the edge of her bed in her white slip. Brit had never owned a slip. If she wore a dress or a skirt, which she didn't, she certainly didn't wear another skirtlike thing under it.

"Guess what," said Nannie, with a wicked little grin. She looked like a Christmas elf turning to crime.

163

Brit couldn't guess her own middle name right now. "What?"

"Guess."

"I can't guess, Nannie." One more minute, she thought, and I'm going to throw myself out the window.

"When Aston was driving along and bragging to his girlfriend on the phone," said Nannie, "guess what I took."

"I give up, Nannie."

"He said *his whole life was in it*. What could we use that has Aston Gibbs's whole life in it?"

"I don't know!" shrieked Brit.

"His laptop. I took it out of his briefcase and put it in the bottom of my handbag and hid it under Flo's wig."

Brit stared at her grandmother.

"A Buttermere," explained Nannie, "does not surrender."

★ ★ ★

By midnight Brit had proved she was no Buttermere. She was totally ready to surrender. She had opened every icon on Aston's desktop. She'd had high hopes for *Mohegan,* a casino in Connecticut, where maybe Aston had lost all the entire million six and they were after him and about to break his kneecaps. But the file contained only performance schedules of featured entertainers. *Nursing Homes* did not say how he planned to make Aurelia hurry up and die, but had comparative data on various institutions. *Retirement,* which ought to have told her how he was frittering away his million six and needed more, contained articles downloaded from the *Wall Street Journal.*

Nannie had tried so hard, snatching Aston's life at the same moment he'd snatched hers. With his computer, she expected her brilliant granddaughter to defeat Aston Gibbs. Brit had failed.

At five minutes after midnight, she picked up her cell phone. Another advantage of cell phones: you could call a person at a crazy hour and nobody else in their family would know. Brit phoned the computer genius she knew best. The one who loved going into other people's private files. Cooper James.

How amazing that Brit had wasted half a year weeping in humiliation because one dumb guy made one dumb gesture. How amazing that she had even cared. Real suffering was what Aurelia was facing, what Nannie had gone through losing those babies, what Flo had gone through losing Lenny.

Coop answered sullenly, which was not surprising at this hour. "Yeah?"

"It's me. Brit."

"I know. I can read."

"I need help."

"Why? So you can hang up on me? You're the most annoying person I've ever known, and I got to know a lot of annoying people when I was getting voted out of existence in that year-book thing."

"*I'm* annoying? *You* stuck your finger down your throat just because you found out that I like you."

"Okay, I'm sorry about the library thing. Your files brought out the seventh grader in me. I got all Rupert-ish and—oh, forget it, Brit. Whatever. It was months ago. What do you want *now*?" He spoke as if Brit never wanted to do anything except bother him and ruin his life.

"I need you," she said. It was hard to breathe. What if he let her down? He might. She didn't actually know Coop—she only wanted to know him. And was he a good reliable person, or did she just want him to be? "You have to pull an all-nighter for me, Cooper. I've got Aston's laptop but I can't find anything incriminating and I'm so tired I can't read any more anyhow. He kidnapped Nannie today. He's a fiend. I don't think I've ever used that word, but he's a fiend, and I'm getting him. Except I can't seem to do it and he's winning. I'm going to download it all to you and you're going to analyze everything and get me what we need before ten a.m., which is when we meet that lawyer." Even to Brit this sounded a little too demanding. "Please," she added.

"He kidnapped Nannie?" repeated Coop.

"She's fine. I got her back. Nothing really happened." Brit told him about everything, except Aston's threats to her. She couldn't say those out loud. It would give them substance. "See, Cooper, I can't stand the thought of Aston jumping up and down and yelling, I won, I won! I'm rich, I'm rich! Plus I'm not really sure Aston and Chloe will even let Aurelia live with Flo."

"You checked his e-mail?" said Coop.

"I don't know his password."

"Professor types are proud to be no good at technology. Proud they can't memorize a password because their minds are full of finer things. Plus I bet he can't believe anybody would touch *his* computer. Probably thinks anything he owns is sacred. I bet he set his online access to bypass his password."

"No way!" said Brit, clicking fast. "You're right, Cooper!"

"Welcome!" cried the computer, which was certainly not what the computer's owner would say. *"You've* got *mail!"* it added, always delighted to stress that the person with the mail was you. The computer was mistaken.

"See if he saves everything," Cooper ordered. "I bet he's got his e-mail on automatic save."

Brit clicked. "Yup. Hundreds of e-mails."

"Forward everything. Get some sleep. I'll call."

But of course she didn't sleep. For one thing, it took forever to forward the stuff. And then she was too wired. But it was all going to work out now. Coop would get something on Aston and they'd nail him. Since Aurelia didn't want to have her own son arrested, Brit and Coop would have him arrested. Flo was pretty decent to take Aurelia in, but even more decent would be for Aurelia to buy her own condo in that retirement village and pay her own bills.

In the morning, Brit would sashay into that meeting and hold up that laptop and taunt him right back: *Guess wha-at I know.*

No.

Better not bring the laptop.

It was stolen.

When the phone rang at four a.m., she could hardly drag herself into consciousness. "Coop," she mumbled. "What do we have?"

"Bad news."

"That's what we want!"

"Bad news for us," said Coop. "I didn't find a thing. Aston is not a nice guy; that's easy to prove. He's promising two different women that he'll marry them. He's promising one of them,

167

the Dr. White you were telling me about, that they'll start a family. But he's got an actual wedding date set with the other woman. Then, his next hobby is, he forwards these poor women's letters to various guys and they write back what a joke it is to use women. So the guy's a lowlife and bragging about it. But being a bum doesn't send you to jail."

"You must have found proof of stealing."

"Nope."

"Fake power of attorney?"

"Couldn't find any reference to it."

"But he sold his mother's house and kept all the money for himself."

"Probably. He definitely gets rich all of a sudden. He buys a yacht and e-mails everybody about it and the timing is about when he sold Aurelia's house. Then he quits his university position, probably because he doesn't need the salary anymore. This one colleague of his? This woman he hates because her book sells and his doesn't? He fakes these really crude e-mails from her and forwards them to the entire faculty. It's probably ruined her."

So Aston had not been bluffing when he said he'd ruin Brit.

She was beaten. They were all beaten. It explained in part why Aurelia hadn't argued more, written more letters, made more phone calls, done a thousand more things to get herself out of Fox Hills. Aston lied well enough to beat them even when they had the laptop that contained his whole life.

"Listen, Brit," said Coop. "Load the car and drive away. Aston is a snake. He's coiling up. You don't want to be in range and you don't want your grandmother in range either, or Aurelia or Flo."

"Aurelia still trusts Chloe."

"Then leave her behind. You and your grandmother go."

168

She was a little shocked. "I have to take care of the girls."

Nannie hated phrases like that. *I don't need taking care of!* she would cry.

And what a stupid pretense that she, Brit, could take care of them. She had signally failed to take care of them. I wanted to drive six white horses, she thought, like the girl who was coming round the mountain, and I can't even find the barn.

"Call the police," said Coop.

"We can't." Brit was still unable to repeat what Aston would say to the police about her. How Aston would love doing it— and how well he'd do it. Way back when she had wanted to be "the Brittany who . . ." she yearned to be "the Brit who dates Coop" or "the Brit who drives the great car." But if Aston talked to the police, she would be "the Brit who preys on the elderly."

★ ★ ★

She slept a little, had a bad dream and woke up feeling thin and weak, as if coming down with the flu. Brit was not a taker of pills or vitamins. She was not a believer in meditation or self-examination. She was a runner.

She put on her jeans and her old sweatshirt. In the jeans pocket she felt the diamond-and-emerald bracelet and this time she pulled it out, enchanted again by its beauty. She ran her fingers over the glittering facets and fastened it on her wrist. At least there was one flawless thing in her existence. Then she got her cell and left the hotel to run the perimeters of the enormous parking lots.

It wasn't too cold that morning. Maybe sixty. In a minute she'd be sweaty.

She ran slowly at first, going around the worst puddles and trying to run over relatively dry areas. She circled the big-box stores way behind the Sheraton and came back along a line of scrubby trees. Way off she could see a tiny airport. She passed the office building where Chandler & Chandler had its ground floor office. How abandoned and gray everything felt, as if nobody else in the world was even awake, never mind at work.

She ran until the sweat was pouring off her and she was at that stage where a person had only one plan: a shower. She kept running, a poster child for throgs' necks.

Perhaps she would run until she dropped.

She avoided the cars, which people had parked as close to the hotel as possible. A handful were scattered farther out. On her fourth pass, she saw a car that had not been there before. A black car, parked away from the rest, all by itself.

A Porsche.

Was it Aston's?

Was he trying to break into Nannie's room, or Brit's, and get his laptop back?

But maybe it wasn't him. People with terrific cars often parked where other cars wouldn't ding them.

Brit walked closer to check the plates.

ASTNIII.

The whole car had been keyed.

Even Brit, who hated Aston and would have loved to drag the sharp vicious edges of her keys down the length of his Porsche, was shocked by the damage to that beautiful finish. Somebody else was just as mad at Aston as she was. Deep gashes ran all the way around the car, and on the hood was a scrawl almost like letters. She touched the damage with her fingers, wondering who had done it. She was afraid of that person too.

Aston laughed.

He was standing maybe twenty feet away, half hidden behind a pickup truck, balancing a large heavy out-of-date video recorder. "I have you on film," he said, smiling. "The way you keyed my car. The way you enjoyed keying my car and came back to stroke your work. The way you keyed your own initials into the hood."

She looked down at her hand, her own fingertips pressing against the slashes. *BAB,* said the vandalism.

"On film," he whispered, smiling.

CHAPTER 14

The wind picked up, turning the sweat on Brit's body to ice.

Aston was cheerful. "We will notify the police, of course. Chloe and I agreed that we can't let you get away with this. We'll see how Mommy and Daddy feel when the police reach them."

The hotel seemed a mile off. And so what if she did run into the hotel? No place was safe. She could maybe have extricated herself from Aston's lies. But this would convict her. By extension, his film would convict her of every other thing he said.

He lowered the heavy video camera. Her eyes followed it, as if following her fate.

"You stole a helpless old woman from the safety of her hospital bed," he said. What pleasure he was taking in repeating the threats. He had her so cornered. "You were told by the aides that her son and her doctor had to give permission, but you sneered at the rule and you snatched her anyway."

"She wanted to go," whispered Brit.

"You stole her jewelry. A witness saw you pocket a bracelet."

Brit could not stop herself from glancing at the wrist clasped by that very bracelet. Aston lifted the video camera again. "Same hand that keyed the car. You really did steal it, didn't you?"

Brit couldn't speak.

"My case was a little thin. But I have you now, Brittany Anne. Vandal and thief on tape. The rest follows. You forced the poor old ladies to stay in cheap motels. You made them skip meals. When my mother begged to see her lawyer, you refused. You went instead."

She was crying. "All you want is Aurelia's money."

"You think anybody will believe you when I play a tape on which you destroy my car, wearing my mother's diamond-and-emerald bracelet, the cherished anniversary gift from my dear father? I think it must have been a twenty-fifth anniversary, don't you? That will touch the judge's heart, won't it?"

In school, they were always insisting that you had options. But what about when you didn't have options? What about when the other side had all the options?

"Wait till your grandmother watches this. She'll have a heart attack from the shock."

"Why are you even doing this?" said Brit. "Why bother with me or my grandmother? We're nothing to you."

"You stood between me and what I want. It was fun shoving that old bat around."

"What you want is for your mother to hurry up and die."

"She can take her time dying now. She doesn't matter anymore. I have the money. That's all that ever mattered."

"At least let Aurelia go to the reunion," begged Brit. "They don't have anything left. It's all been taken from them. And they love Buttermere so."

"She's not going to her reunion. She's returning to Fox Hills."

"Why? What's your point? It would be a kindness to let her have the reunion."

"I need her attorney and her physician to realize how intensely I care about the welfare of my dear old mother. Therefore, I will tuck her back in bed if it takes a straitjacket. Now go get my laptop."

He'd probably tape Brit returning it to him as proof that she'd stolen it. Four days since she'd finished junior year at high school and she was literally finished.

Aston stepped toward her. She flinched at the thought of his touch and gave him a wide berth, trying to reach the hotel without him getting close. He followed her right into the lobby, taping. She headed for the elevator but she was scared to be alone with him in that tiny box, so she took the stairs. Like one of the girls, she hauled herself up by the railings. Aston stayed at the bottom, taping her progress.

She made it to her floor.

Made it to her room.

Dug out the room key.

Unlocked her door.

Slammed it behind her and threw the dead bolt.

She wanted desperately to shower. She couldn't face whatever was coming next when she was smelly and sweaty and dirty. But she was too afraid of Aston to take the time. She hoisted the laptop. Either it was heavy or she was weak.

She stepped out into the corridor.

Cooper James was standing there.

I have a fever, she thought.

Coop was grinning. His T-shirt was plain undershirt white. His jeans were plain denim blue. He had shaved recently. He looked smooth and sporty and safe. She hardly knew him. She couldn't imagine how he had appeared in her hotel hallway. I'm hallucinating, she thought. "You don't drive" was all she could think of to say.

"Nope. But Rupert does. My brother got in last night and he heard me fooling around on the Internet, so he came in and read Aston's e-mails with me."

In her stupor, she had hardly noticed a second person standing there. "I thought you lived in Montana," she said confusedly.

Rupert had not shaved in weeks. His T-shirt was dirtier than Brit's sweatshirt. His jeans were worn at the knees and frayed at the seams. He looked like somebody recently kicked out of a loser rock band trying to make himself feel better with a handful of illegal pharmaceuticals.

He was scary. And awesomely handsome. "Finished college this month," he said, grinning.

The grin was so wild that Brit realized who must have keyed Aston's car: Rupert, in some crazy attempt to help out.

"I was on the six-year plan at college," Rupert told her. "Nobody believed I'd actually finish my classes, let alone pass them and get a degree. I'm home to see the folks before I go all middle class and shave and get a job and pay taxes." Rupert took the laptop from Brit's arms.

"No," she said faintly. "I have to give it to Aston. You don't understand. See—"

"*You* don't understand," said Coop. "See, I get off the phone with you around four in the morning and I'm telling Rupert there's no way to save a person unless you have a car. Rupert says, You really think she needs saving? And I say, Aston's idea of a fun time is shoving eighty-six-year-old ladies around. I tell Rupert, I don't think Brit has a plan, and if she does, it's a stupid one."

Brit could not argue with this viewpoint.

"And me," said Rupert, "I'm always up for interfering in other people's lives, so we never even go to bed. By five, we're in our mother's Volvo wagon and we're hauling up here. We pull into the parking lot just in time to see you run by. You don't see us; you're like all runners; you're inside that zone, whatever it is. I've certainly never found it."

"We park next to the hotel," said Coop, and Brit had the weird sensation of not being able to tell them apart; they were equally adorable, although Coop looked pretty wholesome and Rupert looked pretty evil. "What pulls in a minute later but a black Porsche with vanity plates. ASTNIII. Aston gets out of his car. He has a video recorder. Not state-of-the-art, I might add. Not like my own." Coop held up a palm-sized Sony Micro camcorder. "As you well know, I don't travel down the hall at high school, never mind out of state, without being camera ready. And doesn't Aston *key his own car* while you're running around?"

Aston keyed the Porsche?

"And we tape him," said Rupert, grinning again.

"What do you mean, 'we'?" said Coop. "*I* filmed him. *You* are the chauffeur. You have the driver's license."

"I never claimed to have a license," said Rupert.

Coop stared at his brother. "You don't have a license?"

"Connecticut took mine away for five years, sport. States have reciprocity now. I couldn't just sign up again in Montana. You can shift across the country but you won't be a stranger. Why do you think I took up horses and dirt bikes?"

Brit was laughing helplessly.

Coop said to her, "Brothers. They should stay in Montana where they belong."

"Then you couldn't have come to rescue me," Brit told him. "Except I'm not rescued. You don't know what Aston is going to do to me."

"We do know. We're hunched down behind that red pickup truck over there, see, and Aston is hunched down behind the white pickup over *there,* and he's so happy when you touch that car, he practically wets his pants. We're ready to break his fingers off if he touches you but we let the guy talk. You didn't tell me about those threats, Brit. If I'd known—well, I wanted to kill him right away, but Rupert says, Keep taping, we can kill him later. We didn't get a good picture because we had to tape through the windows of two vehicles. But the audio came out fine."

"The audio?" she whispered, hardly daring to believe.

"We've got his threats on tape," explained Rupert. "And his cute little confession that only the money ever mattered."

"Yes!" shrieked Brit. "We can jail him! Let's call the police!" She did a little stomp dance in the hotel hall.

"I don't do police," Rupert informed her. "Especially in Massachusetts. I have a history here."

"Then what good is the tape? We have to show it to somebody or it's useless."

"Aurelia never wanted the police in on this anyway," Rupert reminded her.

"How do you know so much detail?" said Brit, frowning.

"Coop had to consult somebody," said Rupert. "Little brothers always look to their older brothers for advice and assistance."

"Get out of town," said Coop. "I've survived this long by ignoring your advice. I spent the drive up here weighing in my mind everything you told me, Brit."

Why? she thought. For the adventure of it? To right a wrong? Because you've always wanted to be like Rupert? Because you like me?

"I think Aurelia's right to trust Chloe," said Cooper. "I bet Chloe stayed awake all night feeling guilty because she never visited Aurelia. I bet she's sweating BB pellets that you're right and that power of attorney *is* faked and Aston *did* force his mother into Fox Hills. She has to know that if Aurelia was not competent to run her affairs yesterday, she isn't competent today. And vice versa: if Aurelia can sign away her money today, then she was competent yesterday to run her own affairs. Chloe knows she's not much of a lawyer right now. But I think she wants to be a good lawyer. We're going to give her a way out," said Coop triumphantly.

What does "we" mean? thought Brit. I want "we" to mean "we're a couple now" when of course "we" just means the three people standing here in this corridor.

"We," said Coop, "are going to show Chloe this tape."

★ ★ ★

Chloe watched Cooper's tape. Listened. Watched it again. Then she sighed and met Brit's eyes. "I apologize."

"Good. Here's the outcome we need," said Brit. "We need Aurelia to keep the rest of her money and also her farmhouse in Ashburnham. We need her to be free to live where she wants to live, which is not Fox Hills. We need Aston to sign something promising he'll never get near her or her money again."

Chloe nodded. "And we need to prosecute this Dr. White."

"No, because we're putting Aurelia first. Aurelia loves her son, even though he's rotten to the core. She doesn't want the police, she doesn't want this made public and she doesn't even want it proved. She just wants her reunion. She wants to remember Aston's little red sled and how he was a nice little boy once." Brit looked around the law office. It had the same civilized glossy look it had had the day before. But now both she and Chloe knew that a Burberry raincoat did not make a person civilized.

For Aurelia's sake, however, the ending had to be civilized. "Chloe," said Brit, "in honor of the memory of Woollie, will you represent Aurelia? Will you see that Aurelia gets what she hopes for? Freedom from that institution and freedom from her son's control?" They sounded like wedding vows.

"I will," said Chloe, like a bride, promising before God and these witnesses to keep her vows.

Brit looked at her watch. "The girls still think you're meeting them in the hotel."

"I am meeting them in the hotel," said Chloe, "but I may be late and the agenda has changed."

"When do we get to kill Aston?" asked Cooper. "Is that on the agenda?"

"Killing Aston," said Chloe, "though personally satisfying, would not meet our goals."

"You know, Chloe, you're all right," said Rupert. "Any chance that while you're at it, you could pay somebody off and get my driving record wiped clean?"

"No. Now, here is what we will do. Brit, you will talk to the girls. Show them the tape if you like, or keep it from them if that works better. Aston—" She frowned. "Where exactly did you put him, Rupert?"

"He's in the closet. I don't think he likes it there. But he fit."

Chloe did not complain. "Aston and I will discuss his remaining options. I will telephone the lawyer who created the false power of attorney and the physician who lied about Aurelia's mental capacity. Then I will meet with Aurelia as planned. I will bring the will she asked for. With that signed, the girls can go on to their reunion."

"Want me to stay with you?" said Rupert hopefully. "In case Aston gets rowdy?"

"'Rowdy' is a Montana word," said Chloe. "I cannot imagine Aston Gibbs being rowdy. He might be dangerous, however, so I accept your offer, Rupert. Do stay. Just for effect."

★ ★ ★

The effect was pretty good.

Rupert was back in time to give everybody a status update while Coop got them a table in the hotel dining room for brunch. The maitre d' was scared of Rupert. "It's all right," said Nannie reassuringly. "He's with me."

Coop helped the girls into chairs and found a resting place for Aurelia's all-terrain walker. The boys settled in as if all their best friends were eighty-six years old. They caught on right away that they had to yell. Their yells were a hundred times louder than they needed to be, since when they yelled, they wanted the sound to cross a soccer field, whereas when a normal person yelled, they just wanted to be heard across the table.

"So you single-handedly foiled him," said Aurelia. "My dear Cooper, I thank you so much."

"It was not single-handed," said Rupert. "Both my hands were also involved."

Brit felt a double crush coming on. Thank goodness she had managed a shower and a change of clothes. She was clean and pretty and she liked her hair and even felt smart enough for calculus.

"I knew something like this would happen, Britsy," said Nannie with satisfaction. "I knew we would win. Buttermeres never surrender."

"I'm not a Buttermere," Brit pointed out. "And even if I go to your college, I can't be a Buttermere because they tore it down."

"You're a Buttermere," said Nannie with certainty.

Even having all your marbles did not approach the magnificence of such a compliment. To be a Buttermere was to be the best.

Flo offered to pay for brunch, and everybody was courteous and accepted, especially the boys, who had already taken gas money from Flo for the trip home. "There's only one detail left," said Flo.

"The bracelet," said Brit, undoing the clasp and holding it out to Aurelia. "Really and truly, it just happened to be there."

Aurelia laughed. "Darling, it was meant to glitter on a young girl's wrist. Let me give it to you. Such small thanks for such great help."

"Oh, Aurelia, I'm in love with diamonds and emeralds now, but I don't want this. I'd always have to think of the bad stuff."

"I fully comprehend," said Aurelia. "Perhaps we should give it to the poor."

"I'm poor," said Rupert hopefully.

Flo took control of the bracelet. "Fortunately I still chair a hospital board," she said. "I'll decide who's poor." Flo was beautifully dressed, accessorized, bejeweled and, once again, bewigged. She looked like a million dollars. Which, it occurred to Brit, she was. "No, the final detail is this," said Flo. "Who is going to drive the last leg of the journey to the reunion?"

"I am," said Brit, offended.

"No. You've seen enough of old ladies. You deserve a real summer. I telephoned my son George, who always comes through in the end. He and Danielle will be here this afternoon. Danielle will take us to our reunion. George will take you home in the rental car, Brit, and return it for you."

"What? I haven't even met Daisy! You're kicking me out? I was a perfectly good driver in the end! I was a pretty good driver at the beginning too."

The girls looked as if they might argue that point.

"I called Hayley," said Nannie. "I explained that you need to stay with her for a few days. Hayley is getting people to cover for her at Dairy Queen because she needs to be home so you can talk forty-eight hours straight and tell her every single thing that happened."

You guys keep weighing me down with this stuff and I'm going to need a walker of my own, she had said to Flo. *Or friends,* Flo had replied. I have friends, thought Brit. She looked at Coop and thought, What's he doing here, anyway? Getting your brother to drive you out of state to check on some girl . . . That's seriously beyond friendship. That's . . . what?

Whatever it was, she didn't want it to happen on a cell phone.

She wanted it in person. Preferably persons squished up really close to each other.

"I don't know every single thing that happened either," said Coop. "Can I sit in on this?"

"Don't leave me out," said Rupert.

"It's a high school thing," Coop told his brother. "You're old. You're ready for reunions of your own. But hey, I've got a great idea, Brit. Why don't you drive back to Connecticut with *us*? Let this guy George return the rental car up here."

"But neither one of you," Brit said worriedly, "has a—"

Cooper and Rupert glared at her.

"Right," said Brit. "Nannie?"

"Yes, darling?"

"Why don't I drive back to Connecticut with Coop and Rupert?"

"I don't know, darling. What would your parents say?"

"I don't know, Nannie. What are they going to say about the yard and the rental car and the kidnapping and the laptop theft?"

Nannie giggled. "Perhaps on your drive home with Cooper and Rupert, you can work that out. I don't want any blame, darling. You take it all on your strong young shoulders."

Brittany Anne Bowman looked at her double crush. Talk about strong young shoulders.

She was laughing; the girls were laughing; Coop and Rupert were laughing.

I won, I won, thought Brit. I'm rich, I'm rich.

Rich the way it counts: in friends.

CAROLINE B. COONEY is the author of *Diamonds in the Shadow; A Friend at Midnight; Hit the Road; Code Orange; The Girl Who Invented Romance; Family Reunion; Goddess of Yesterday* (an ALA Notable Book); *The Ransom of Mercy Carter; Tune In Anytime; Burning Up; The Face on the Milk Carton* (an IRA-CBC Children's Choice Book) and its companions, *Whatever Happened to Janie?, The Voice on the Radio* (each of them an ALA Best Book for Young Adults), and *What Janie Found; What Child Is This?* (an ALA Best Book for Young Adults); *Driver's Ed* (an ALA Best Book for Young Adults and a *Booklist* Editors' Choice); *Among Friends; Twenty Pageants Later;* and the Time Travel Quartet: *Both Sides of Time, Out of Time, Prisoner of Time,* and *For All Time.*

Caroline B. Cooney lives in Madison, Connecticut, and New York City.